KU-500-939

THE HIGH RIDERS

In the Bighorn Mountains of Wyoming, Bodie is on the trail of Lew Gallman and his gang — a bunch of brutes who'll go to any lengths to get what they want, and kill anyone who stands in their way. Tracking them into the heart of a raging storm, Bodie takes shelter in a cave, and meets Ruby Kehoe — the survivor of an encounter with the Gallman crew, which left her wounded and her companions dead . . .

NEIL HUNTER

THE
HIGH RIDERS

Complete and Unabridged

LINFORD
Leicester

First published in Great Britain in 2016

First Linford Edition
published 2018

Copyright © 2016 by Michael R. Linaker
All rights reserved

A catalogue record for this book is available
from the British Library.

ISBN 978–1–4448–3758–2

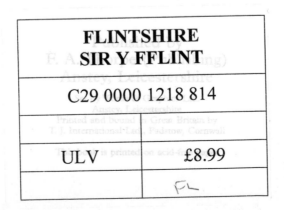

FLINTSHIRE SIR Y FFLINT	
C29 0000 1218 814	
ULV	£8.99
	FL

1

Bighorn Mountains, Wyoming Territory

It was a known fact — Bodie did not like rain. Especially the driving, chilled downpour he was forced to ride through as he negotiated the rocky slopes of the Bighorn Mountains. And this part of the country appeared to be suffering one hell of a stormy period. The rain had persisted over the last couple of days as the manhunter tracked the men he was after: a merciless bunch who were wanted for a continued cycle of robberies and murder.

Five of them. Josh Stringer. Lang Wilkerson. Joe Lagrange. Ramon Vasquez. And Lew Gallman, the man who led the gang.

Bodie had picked up their trail north of Laramie, finding he was about three days behind them as they pushed their way through Wyoming and left behind a string of broken banks and equally broken bodies. The Gallman bunch had a particularly nasty habit of gunning down anyone who got in their way, or supposedly got in their way. Regard for human life did not seem to be in their makeup. They were as cold-blooded a bunch Bodie had ever come across. He had already set himself for a bloody confrontation when he met up with them, and in his mind had decided this was going to end up with his quarry more dead than alive. Cold comfort for the recent victims if that did happen, but Bodie didn't set the rules. He simply went down the road that would leave him standing at the conclusion.

He drew rein, easing his horse under a canopy of branches that at least slowed the downpour. He hunched his slicker closer. His horse was a strong chestnut mare with a propensity to sulkiness when the weather didn't suit. She disliked the rain as much as Bodie, and displayed her mood by snorting loudly and jerking against the bit.

'Ain't my damn fault it's raining,' Bodie said. 'Just the way it is, so quit jigging about.'

From where he was sheltering, Bodie could see beyond the rise of ground to where the craggy slopes stepped up to misty peaks. From the route the Gallman bunch was moving, he figured they were making for them.

The High Lonesome. The isolated slopes where a man could lose himself, surrounded by rocky escarpments and meadows. Places a man could hide and not be found if he really didn't care to be. Bodie had spent some time in the past up in the high peaks when he'd been in need of a break. There were times a man took to the empty spaces while he cleared his head and lived the simple life, away from people and their attendant complications.

He felt the mare moving under him, restless and still unsettled. 'Okay, horse, I hear you.'

He worked the reins and eased the

chestnut out from beneath the trees, picking up the trail again. The down-pour pounded his sodden hat and rolled off the enveloping slicker. The fall was heavy enough that it created a silvery mist when it hit the ground.

It was barely mid-morning, with a long day stretching out in front of Bodie. He had spent the previous night sheltering beneath a moss-covered over-hang large enough to take him and his horse. It had been an uncomfortable night. The rocky ground underneath had left him stiff and in an unsociable mood; which, given his situation, wasn't entirely unexpected. A cold meal had done little to make him feel better. Even thinking about the bounties being offered for the Gallman gang did little to ease his discomfort.

Overhead, Bodie picked up the low rumble of thunder over the distant peaks. It promised more rain and the likelihood of a storm.

'And you think you've got something to grumble about,' Bodie said to the chestnut. 'Hell, you figure you're wet now. Wait till that storm hits.'

His warning came to fruition less than an hour later when the increasing rumble of thunder became intense. The deep boom preceded the increase in the downpour. The rain hit with physical force, and Bodie hunched his shoulders against it. On the higher peaks, strikes of lightning flashed, brilliant jagged fingers crisscrossing the uppermost escarpments. Bodie felt the mare balk, nervous tremors shaking the animal. He held the reins taut, then leaned over, stroking the powerful neck and using gentle words to calm her. He could understand the chestnut's agitation. The sight and sound of a full-strength mountain storm could unnerve the steadiest human, let alone an already fidgety horse. It took Bodie a couple of fraught minutes to fetch the animal under control, and though she still didn't like it, she kept moving forward.

The dense clouds turned the day gloomy, making it harder for Bodie to stay on his course. He was determined to keep his marker in sight: a particular-shaped peak he was using to maintain his line of travel. It was his only point of reference in this unknown country. Bodie had no maps, no written directions. All he had were his tracking skills, and the instinct developed from years of using them.

'Horse, I'm feeling sorry for myself right now. Weather like this makes a feller downright moody.'

The chestnut, head down against the storm, made no response. It simply plodded forward through the rain.

'Getting to you as well, huh? Well, we're a sorry pair.'

A bright flash of lightning lit up the area. In the stark brilliance, Bodie caught a glimpse of a dark cave mouth off to his left, a wide gap in the face of a rising rock wall, water streaming down the open hole. He eased the chestnut round and pushed it up the stony bank fronting the high face. It was no welcoming manmade structure, but it might at least provide some degree of shelter from the drenching storm, and he was in no position to be too picky.

He dismounted and took the reins, leading his horse up to the cave, negotiating the loose slope and splashing through the watery overspill. A few feet inside, the interior was shadowed. Not completely dark, but gloomy enough to prevent Bodie from seeing the human shape in time to back off.

The shape moved forward, low light enough to reflect off the metal of a rifle that was aimed directly at him, the muzzle settling on a point between his belt buckle and his chest.

2

He was aware of his own vulnerability, accepting that one day he might be caught unawares.

Bodie's maudlin thought of only a few minutes ago came back as he eyed the unwavering rifle muzzle. He hadn't expected it to happen quite so fast.

'I could shoot you right now if I had a mind.'

The voice was tight with caution. It was also female, and Bodie detected a slight unease.

'I'm not about to argue that point,' he said. 'And I ain't about to give you any reason to prove it. Right now, all I want is to get in out of this damned rain. My horse and I stay out here much longer, we'll just get washed away. Or struck by lightning. Be obliged if we could take cover, is all.'

The indistinct figure stepped forward,

the targeted rifle staying on Bodie. He saw a well-shaped young woman clad in man's clothing, her auburn hair tumbling in thick coils to her shoulders. Her pale face, with strong cheekbones and a firm-set mouth, was startlingly beautiful. Her searching gaze, from hazel eyes, examined Bodie's tall figure as if that look would tell her everything she would ever want to know about him. He figured her to be in her late twenties.

At any other moment in time, Bodie would have allowed himself to appreciate her beauty from a strictly male point of view. But instead he concentrated on the damp bloodstain showing through the fabric of her gray shirt on her right side. From the freshness of the patch, it was obvious the wound was still bleeding. Her clothing was untidy, cut and torn, just as her face and hands were. She had a bruise on one cheek.

'Ma'am, you've been hurt some.'

'Not enough to stop me pulling this trigger.'

'I don't doubt it, but I figure you

doing that wouldn't be too good for either of us.'

'A bullet for you.'

'No question there. But the way you're holding that Winchester against your wound isn't the smart thing to do. That gun is going to kick it hard. Not the best thing for you. Ain't about to do a deal for your healing.'

She dropped her eyes for a moment to glance at the wound. In those brief few seconds, Bodie lunged forward, left hand reaching out to push the rifle's muzzle out of harm's way, followed by the right to snatch the weapon from her grasp. The woman made a grab to regain control, but the sudden move drew a gasp of pain from her lips and she hurriedly clamped both hands to her side, bending forward against the hurt. Bodie reached out with his empty left hand to grip her shoulder and take some of her weight.

'Easy now,' he said. 'Take it easy, ma'am. Let's not go getting too excited.'

Bodie laid the rifle down and guided her to the side of the cave, his big hands gentle. He helped her to sit. She offered no resistance.

'You have anything with you?'

The auburn hair swayed as she shook her head. 'Just me and the rifle.'

'Sit tight, then.'

Bodie went to his horse and led it all the way inside the cave. He shrugged out of the slicker, then went to his roll behind the saddle wrapped in an oilcloth, and freed it. He shook out his blankets and wrapped them around the woman's shoulders. She grasped the sides and pulled the blankets around her.

'Thank you,' she said.

Bodie brought his canteen and offered it to her. She drank sparingly, leaning her head against the cave wall.

'I'm hoping you don't have anything to do with those men.'

Bodie wondered how many more surprises the day was going to bring. 'Not *with* them,' he said. 'More like following them.'

The woman pulled the blankets tighter around her, the hazel-flecked eyes searching his face. 'A lawman?'

'Used to be a long time back. Now I do it for the money.'

A frown creased her forehead. Then she said, 'Bounty man.'

Bodie noticed she didn't make it sound grubby. 'It's a dirty job, but somebody has to do it,' he said, trying for lightness.

'I'd need a lot of money to go chasing those . . . ' She hesitated. 'I almost used an unladylike word.'

'It sounds as if you have a story to tell.'

'If you have the time.'

Bodie glanced out the cave entrance at the torrential rain that was showing no sign of slackening off. 'We could be here for a spell.'

'I'm Ruby Kehoe.'

'Bodie.' He produced a few strips of beef jerky from his saddlebag pouch. 'You hungry?'

Ruby reached out and took a strip. 'Right now, that looks good.'

'Those men who met up with you. How many?'

'Five. I heard one of them use a name. He called one of them Stringer.'

'Josh Stringer. That would make them the bunch I'm trailing. The Gallman gang. A rough crowd.'

'I think I could attest to that.'

Her voice faltered and she bent her head, concentrating on chewing the tough meat. Bodie sensed the subject was hard for her. He allowed her time to consider the matter.

'They caught us. Came out of nowhere and said they were taking our horses. They just shot Grant and Rafer, our guide . . . I mean, they shot them without a thought. I can't forget the look in Grant's eyes as the bullets hit him. He fell against me, pushed his rifle in my hand and told me to run. It was the last thing he said to me. I can't even recall how I did get away. We were camped near some trees and brush, so I

13

simply ran. I didn't think. Then those men started shooting. I could hear bullets hitting the trees around me. I fell a couple of times. Got up and ran again. They kept shooting, and I felt something hit my side. By then I was in a total panic; I had no idea where I was going. And then suddenly the shooting stopped, but I didn't . . . I just kept moving until I was so exhausted I simply collapsed. I crawled into the brush and hid. I was terrified, expecting those men to show up at any moment. Then it started to rain, and I realized I needed shelter. I found this place. Been here ever since, trying to work out what to do next.'

'What were you people doing up here?'

'Seems so stupid now. Grant was my cousin. We came here so he could take photographs. He worked for a magazine in New York. They commissioned him to create a portfolio of the Western mountains. Pictures, maps. I was his work partner. My job was to write the words to accompany his illustrations. This wasn't the first time we collaborated. California, Oregon, the Eastern states. A couple of years ago we did one on Canada. Grant had always wanted to do something here. He loved the idea of the mountains. The forests . . . '

She broke off suddenly, cupping her hands to her face, and Bodie saw her shoulders shaking. 'You've had a rough time,' he said.

Ruby looked directly at him. 'What do I do now? Everything's gone. Grant, my cousin. The man we hired to guide us, Rafer Bledsoe. Both dead. Those men took our horses, even the pack animal with all Grant's equipment. Food, supplies, it's all gone. Mr. Bodie, I have nothing left to survive on.'

'For what it's worth, you've got me.'

'But I can't expect you to burden yourself that way. You came up here looking for those men, not to be nursemaid to a woman.'

Bodie appreciated her feelings, and if he'd been so inclined, could have agreed. He had a reputation as a hard man; someone who could walk away if something — or someone — interfered with his situation. And there was a whole lot of truth in that. He was a bounty hunter. His work brought him into contact with some of the worst men around, and he had long ago realized that in order to stand up to those men, he had to be as tough, if not tougher, than any of them. He had a dedicated streak that kept him on the trail of wanted men until he caught up with them. There was something in Bodie's makeup that pushed him forward, never even contemplating backing off. In Bodie's world, quitting didn't exist. That stubborn nature had earned him the title he heard men use about him. Not something he ever uttered, but something he carried like an invisible mark. The Stalker.

That was the persona he widely presented to the world. But it was not the complete person. Faced with the young Ruby Kehoe, he had to offer her

16

some kind of way out of her current situation. He might not have been entirely happy with it; yet there was no way he could simply ride out and leave her here, alone, with nothing but the clothes she stood up in and a single rifle to protect herself — provided she could use the weapon. But the feeling he got was that she would be proficient.

The Gallman bunch was moving away with every passing moment; something else Bodie wasn't pleased about. He had his thoughts, and passed on them. In the immediate moment, there was nothing he could do about that situation, so grumbling about it was not about to change anything. He'd lost quarry before, and always caught up with them later, so he shouldered that and moved on. His priority was the woman.

'I'm holding you back,' Ruby said.

'I would have most likely lost them in this weather.'

She managed a smile at that. 'Mr. Bodie, you are not a very good liar. I'm going to make you lose those men.'

'Only for a while. I'll pick up their trail later.'

'After you get me off your hands.'

'Miss Kehoe, I'll see to it you get to safety. I'm not about to leave you here alone.'

'Thank you. Propriety aside, in our present situation I would rather we did away with formal manners. My name is Ruby.'

'That's fine.'

'And you are?'

'Bodie.'

'Is that first or last?'

'Just Bodie.'

'Rather enigmatic. But I must say it suits you.'

'You warm enough with those blankets?'

'I am — Bodie.'

She watched him cross to stand just inside the opening, staring out at the heavy rain, hands resting lightly on his lean hips. Her eyes were drawn to the holstered pistol resting below his waist.

The weapon looked large and heavy, yet he moved as if he wasn't carrying it around with him. There was nothing fancy in the rig he carried it in, and she realized that to him it was simply a tool of his trade. She noted the thin rawhide that held the holster to his thigh, keeping it steady even when he moved, and she was unable to prevent the question forming in her mind: *How many men has he killed?*

Those outlaws. Desperadoes who lived with Wanted posters hanging over them. Ruby Keogh had heard about those kinds of men. Had read about them. Had listened to the stories. But until the moment those five had forced themselves into her life, she had never contemplated being confronted by them. It had left her shocked — especially to see Grant and Rafer shot down in front of her. Reality was far removed from the reportage in newspapers and magazines. The violence had been shocking to her, the deaths ugly. And she might have remained transfixed if

19

Grant, forcing out the words from suddenly bloody lips, had not pushed his rifle into her hands and used his dying breath to tell her to go. He had stood between Ruby and the killers, hanging on to life and giving her the vital seconds she needed to turn about and run, plunging into the thick brush at her back, ignoring the yelling voices behind. By the time they had reacted, raising their weapons, she had forced her way into the dense brush. She had heard shots, the snap and thud as bullets followed her, and she had thought she would get away untouched until the burning sensation as one bullet tore across her side. If anything, it had forced her to run faster, ignoring the brush that clawed at her, tearing her clothes, leaving her skin scratched and bloody.

Ruby exorcised the images from her thoughts, returning to the moment and her consideration of the man, Bodie, who had come into her life. He was by his own admission a bounty hunter. A man who made his living from going up against others. She had only known him for an extremely short time, yet she felt no fear where he was concerned. It might have been foolish, but she felt safe in his presence.

'I need to see to that wound,' Bodie said abruptly. 'Clean it so it doesn't get infected.'

'I suppose in your line of work, dealing with such things is normal.'

'I never see getting shot as normal.'

'Bad choice of words.'

Bodie had brought over his saddle-bags and was opening them. She watched his capable movements as he took out a small jar, a roll of clean cotton strips, and a squat bottle of what she realized from the label was whisky. He became aware of her scrutiny and held up the bottle.

'Medicinal use.'

'Is that external, or internal?'

'Times are when it can be both. Can you lift your shirt? Let me take a look.'

She did what he asked, pulling up her

shirt until she had exposed the wound. A soft gasp escaped her lips when the cloth had to be tugged away from her flesh. While she did that, Bodie tipped some whisky on his hands and rubbed them together. He peered at the wound: a four-inch surface lesion that had left a wet score in her white flesh. He poured more whisky on a strip of cloth.

'Gonna hurt some,' he said. He held out the bottle. 'You want a bite of whisky?'

'Under the circumstances, why not?'

The liquor slid down her throat, burning all the way. It brought tears to her eyes, and she found it hard to breathe for a few seconds.

While she was fighting off the bitter taste, Bodie worked quickly, cleaning the wound and drying it with a fresh pad of cloth. His touch was sure, and it convinced her this was not the first time he had dealt with such matters. She bit back an exclamation when even his light touch caused a flash of pain.

'You were right, it did hurt, but thank

you for your consideration.'

He worked quickly, forming a pad to cover the wound after applying some of the salve from the jar, then deftly wrapping a long strip of cloth around her slim body and tying it off.

'Need to get a doctor to check that later,' he said, pulling her shirt back down.

'I suppose there are plenty of those in the area.'

He gazed at her, not sure whether she was being serious or not. Then his quick smile came again. 'They teach you these clever remarks at some fancy school back East?'

This time it was Ruby who smiled. 'Bodie, we are going to get along, I believe.'

After he had put his saddlebags back on the horse, he passed her the canteen again. She weighed it in one hand, the bottle of whisky in the other, glancing up at him.

'I'd go for the water,' he said. 'Too much whisky on an empty stomach isn't the best idea.'

'You're right there.'

She passed him the bottle, and he packed it away while she took a drink from the canteen. 'Do you know this part of the country?'

'Not well,' he said. 'Just general knowledge. I was letting the Gallman bunch guide me. Now they do know their way around here. Seems they've ridden these hills on more than one occasion. I'm working on the idea they might have some kind of base camp in the vicinity. Place they go when they need to rest up.'

'If that's so, why doesn't the law go after them in force?'

'That's not as easy as it might sound. This is lonely country. Big, wide country. Pretty isolated. Not many people around. Bunch like the Gallmans depends on that. Out here, the law doesn't mean much. It will one day, when the place gets settled, but right now not many men would sign up to try and flush the Gallman bunch out.

They're liable to sit pretty and pick off anyone blundering around easy as shooting bottles off a fence.'

'You mean like us?'

'They get pretty territorial. Don't favor anyone in their backyard, and turn nasty if someone shows up.'

'Well, I don't want to appear ungrateful, Bodie, but my feelings are for us getting well clear of this place before they decide we're here.'

'You'll get no arguments from me on that,' Bodie said. 'Sooner I can get you to a safe place, the easier I'm going to be.'

'I must be a real burden for you.'

'No offence, Ruby, but I would be a damn sight happier if you weren't here.'

'I understand. Really, I do . . . and I'm sorry I've put you in this situation.'

'Don't get me wrong; it's your health I'm concerned about. Sooner we get you back somewhere safe . . . '

He went back and stared out of the cave mouth, trying to work out how much longer the rainstorm might hold.

The amount of water being dropped across the slopes was heavy. It would make travel difficult. Loose soil and rocks could be treacherous underfoot. Runoffs of excess rain would create unexpected streams cascading down from the high ground. Bodie had even seen trees uprooted as heavy rainfall weakened their roots. Had he been on his own, he might have taken his chances; but with the woman, matters became that much more risky. He didn't doubt Ruby Kehoe to be anything but competent, but she would find travel under such extreme conditions hard.

Bodie glanced over his shoulder and saw her struggling with the strip of jerky he'd provided. That was another problem — a lack of proper food would tell eventually. A human body needed the strength that food provided. It offered fuel to keep a person going. Without it, the body would slow down and lose its capacity to fight off fatigue. In the rugged mountain terrain, that could be fatal. It didn't always take a bullet to bring someone down.

'Any sign that rain starts to slow down, we move,' he said. 'Three, four hours, it'll be dark. Sooner we get moving, the better chance we have. Don't want to be wandering around at night.'

'Just tell me when. It's not as if I have much to pack.'

Bodie picked up her rifle and checked it over. He ejected the full load, part-stripped the weapon, then put it back together. He did it with an ease that came from total familiarity. Ruby watched him thumb the bullets back in and lean it against the cave wall.

'Nice gun,' he said. 'Well looked-after.'

'It was Grant's. He took it with him wherever we went. He never had to use it once, but he said it always came down to the one time you might need it . . . ' Her voice caught, and Bodie saw the gleam of tears in her eyes. She cleared her throat. 'But when that day did come, he didn't even get his chance to protect us.'

'He would have stood no chance against those men, Ruby. They're killers with little respect for others. Grant might have hesitated, but they wouldn't. Taking life doesn't worry them at all. It's the way they operate. Taking from others because they're too damn lazy to work. It's the easy way for them.'

'I hope we don't run into them again.'

'Have to agree with that thought.'

'Hey, *amigo*, I'm sorry to disappoint you, then.'

Bodie turned, dropping his hand to his Colt; but when he saw the rifle aimed at him, held by the slicker-clad man standing at the cave mouth, he knew he had to act quickly.

3

'The pistol. On the ground. Left hand.'

The accent was Mexican. The grinning face one Bodie had seen before. On Wanted flyers.

Ramon Vasquez. One of Gallman's bunch. As mean and hard-faced as the rest. A man with total disregard for anyone, save himself and the men he rode with.

Bodie lifted his Colt and placed it on the ground.

'*Hombre*, I know who you are. The one they call the Stalker. Bodie. Big mean bounty man. Not so smart you could fool Vasquez. I knew you were following us. So I double back and find your tracks. Trail you right here.' He stared beyond Bodie to where Ruby crouched with her back to the cave wall. The grin widened when he recognized her. 'And, *hombre*, you have found our missing woman. We thought she had vanished.'

'Were you worried about me?' Ruby asked, her voice low.

Bodie had seen the flicker of movement in the Mexican's eyes as he focused on Ruby. Saw the slight move of Vasquez's gun muzzle. It angled away from Bodie. He knew it would quickly return to cover him again.

He had his moment. His paper-thin chance. And took it.

Bodie's right hand streaked across his body, fingers closing over the hilt of the big knife sheathed on his left side. He slid the knife free, swept it up and back, and launched it in a smooth blur of movement.

Vasquez jerked his rifle back into line, finger squeezing the trigger. The cave magnified the sound of the shot. The .44–40 slug cleared Bodie's shoulder by a fraction, slammed into the hard rock behind him and spat off with a whine, leaving a white scar behind.

There was no second shot. The rifle

slipped from the Mexican's grip as he reached up to claw at the knife buried in his throat. He tried to pull it free, but the warm blood around the cold steel in his flesh made his fingers slippery. His eyes stared in silent terror. Vasquez slid to his knees.

Bodie retrieved his pistol. He moved forward and kicked Vasquez's rifle aside. As he did, Vasquez toppled on his side, body jerking in spasms.

Behind Bodie there was a soft groan from Ruby.

'Him or us,' Bodie said. 'No debate.'

'I see that, but it . . . '

Bodie picked up the discarded rifle, then bent over Vasquez and reached under the slicker. He found the holstered pistol and took it. 'Now we have extra guns,' he said.

He handed the nickel-plated Colt to Ruby and propped the rifle next to hers. She watched him work his slicker back on. About to ask what he was doing, she realized he was going out to locate the Mexican's horse.

'If anyone who's not me shows up, you know what to do.'

Ruby eased back the hammer on the pistol. 'Just make sure you announce yourself, Mr. Bodie.'

* * *

He was back within a half-hour, leading a handsome black stallion that carried a fancy Mexican saddle on its sleek back. The thirty minutes he had been gone had seemed like hours as Ruby sat, barely taking her eyes from the cave entrance. The sheeting rain reduced her range of vision to a few yards, and all she could make out were the trees and brush bending under the downpour.

Bodie's tall figure materialized out of the storm, rain spilling from the gleaming slicker, the black horse walking quietly behind him. He led the animal alongside his own, stripped off his slicker, and shook water off his sodden hat.

'Miss me?' he said.

'Well, I had nothing else to do.'

'Sooner we leave, the better chance we have of avoiding Vasquez's friends. Problem is, if they figure he's been gone too long, they might backtrack.'

'I was wondering about that myself.'

Bodie checked over the black. He opened the saddlebags and found a couple of canvas bags holding gold coins. He showed them to Ruby. 'They were busy fellers,' he said.

'Do you think they might have killed in order to take those?'

'Going on their past record, it wouldn't surprise me.' He weighed the heavy bags in his hands, turned, and threw them aside.

'What are . . . '

'Lightening the load that black has to carry.'

Bodie picked up his slicker and pulled it on. Crossing to where Vasquez lay, he first pulled his knife from the man's throat, sheathed it, then dragged off the slicker the man was wearing. Ruby watched as he stepped outside and let the rain wash the blood off the garment. He turned and came back inside, holding out the slicker. Ruby might have protested. Instead, she took the slicker and pulled it on, letting it hang. She tucked the pistol he'd given her behind her belt.

When Bodie made to pick up the hat that had fallen from the Mexican's head, she held up a warning hand. 'Oh, no — I won't wear that thing. I prefer to get my head wet,' she said.

Bodie jammed the rifle she had brought with her into the black's saddle boot. She took the reins from him and mounted the horse with ease, leaning forward to stroke its powerful neck. She spoke to it softly, and the animal tossed its head and stood passively.

'He'll do,' Bodie said. He mounted the chestnut, then led the way out of the cave and into the rain.

Beyond the nearby hills, thunder still rumbled and lightning flashed. Heavy weather that showed no sign of letting up.

Ruby eased the black in behind Bodie as they moved through the trees. As safe as she felt in his company, she still carried a sense of unease that suggested the way ahead would be far from peaceful.

4

'If Ramon was right and we have someone on our tails, maybe it's why he ain't got back to us. Happen he found who it was, and happen he's dead.'

The four of them were in their saddles, bunched close. The horses they had taken were with them. Rain bounced off the gleaming black slickers the men wore and pushed their hats against their skulls.

Lang Wilkerson had voiced what they were all thinking. He stared at the others, his thin face showing unshaven cheeks. Wilkerson tended to vocalize the thoughts of the group. He understood what their minds were telling them, and he put this into words.

'You know I make sense. That Mex may be a pain in the ass, but he don't do nothin' for nothin's sake. Time he's been gone ain't right.'

The man next to him stirred in his saddle. It was almost like watching the side of the mountain move. Joe Lagrange was big. Not fat. Big in the sense he was six foot four in height, and at times could have been the same width-wise. An intimidating man with an unfortunately coarse face that only served to make him even more fearsome. He always dressed in heavy clothing that magnified his size, and a wide-brimmed hat pulled low over his mass of dark collar-length hair.

'We should go look for him, Lew,' he said. Lagrange was a man of few words. When he spoke, his voice was quietly commanding. 'He may be in trouble.'

Lew Gallman, a tall man himself, swatted rainwater from his unshaven face. He glanced at the other members of the group. They nodded in silent agreement.

'Fine,' he said. 'Let's go.'

They turned their horses around and headed back the way they had come. They all knew the area and needed no maps to guide them. It took them nigh on two hours to reach the spot where Vasquez had cut off from them.

'He rode that way,' Lagrange said. 'I know'd where he was going. Big cave a few miles back that way. If that woman found it, she'd use it for shelter.'

'Hell, Joe, that's some guess. For all we know, that bitch coulda fell down a ravine and killed herself.'

That was Josh Stringer, the grumbler of the gang. He had a sour nature at the best of times, and being in the heart of the rainstorm brought out the worst in him. A gray-haired boney man in his late forties, Stringer had a nasty streak that allowed him to inflict violence on others without a shred of humanity. He had a patch over his left eye that only added to his air of menace; he had lost his eye many years ago as the end result of a bar fight with an equally brutal man named Sublette. Though Sublette had walked away that day with no more than superficial cuts, he had left Stringer minus one of his eyes. A broken bottle had done that. Stringer had never forgotten. Two years later, he had met with Sublette along the Wind River and had taken his revenge by overpowering the man and, using the heated blade of his knife, burning out *both* of the other man's eyes.

'That would be a damn shame,' Lang Wilkerson said. 'That was some good-looking woman.'

Wilkerson fancied himself a ladies' man. Gangly and prematurely balding, he was far from handsome, but imagined he held some kind of allure for the opposite sex. He was wrong, and when it was pointed out to him — usually by a woman — he got angry and struck out with his fists as if it would prove his masculinity. His temper was short and he never knew when to stop. It had got him into trouble on many an occasion. Wilkerson had a natural aptitude for the gun he carried, and no problem using it.

'Hell, Lang, if that gal saw you staring at her, wouldn't be no surprise if she jumped off a cliff herself,' Lagrange said, laughing at his own remark.

Wilkerson stared at the man riding alongside him, his thin lips curling in a sneer. He didn't say anything, just stared as if he was expecting Lagrange to curl up and die; though if the occasion arose, he would have stood side by side with the man in order for them both to survive.

*   *   *

Lagrange led them through the downpour with the unerring confidence of a tracker dog, picking up the pace once he had his trail set. It was as if he was following a marked route. The others fell in behind him, silent, shoulders hunched against the falling rain, ignoring the rumbling thunder and flickering lightning.

They were, to a man, tough and uncompromising, yet between them they carried a loyalty to each other that

40

was hard to match. They stood aside from others, cut off from society because of how they behaved. Yet within the group there was an unspoken bond that kept them together. A closeness of need. Each depended on the others, and they rode with that unspoken tie that never needed to be uttered.

Lagrange reined in. He pointed through the trees to where a mass of rock thrust into the sky.

'Up there. The cave.'

'You sure?' Gallman asked.

'I'm sure. I'll go take a look.'

'Josh, go with him,' Gallman said.

The pair dismounted, handing over their reins, and started off through the trees, Lagrange in the lead and moving like a man half his size. Stringer followed, hunched over. The shale slope was running with water, leaving the surface loose and unstable. The big man went up surefooted, leaving his partner behind to struggle. He could hear Stringer cursing as he slipped and slid on the slope.

Reaching level rock, Lagrange examined the wide cave mouth in front of him. He thrust a hand under his slicker and gripped the butt of his handgun. He peered around him until he was satisfied, then walked inside the cave.

When Stringer reached the spot, he was confronted by Lagrange as the man came out of the cave. He was holding the canvas bags of stolen money in his hands.

'Ramon's inside,' he said. 'He's dead. Someone stuck a knife in his throat. He done bled all over the cave floor.'

Stringer walked into the cave. He looked down at the body, noticing the extent of the wound. Glancing around, he saw Vasquez's rifle still leaning against the cave wall. He picked it up and took it with him, then showed it to Lagrange.

'One thing's for certain,' Stringer said, 'it was no woman killed Ramon.'

'You see the hoofmarks in there? More than one horse. Ramon said someone was on our back trail.'

'Lawdog?'

'Mebbe. Or a bounty man.'

'So what happened?'

'I'm no Indian. I don't get visions.'

'Hell, Joe, a fuckin' guess is all we need.'

'I imagine the woman found the cave, took shelter, and our man found her. Then Vasquez showed up. They had at it and Vasquez lost. They took his horse and headed back down the mountain.'

'They left the money.'

'Didn't want the weight slowing them down.'

'Well damnit, Joe, they can't have gotten far.'

Stringer made for the exit, Lagrange slower as he followed. He stood outside, eyes raised to the sky where the light was starting to show through the rain. It was slackening off. He could feel the intensity fading. The storm was moving on. Give it an hour or so and the rain would be gone. He heard Stringer cursing as he slipped and slithered down the slope. Lagrange tucked the money bags under his arms and started on down himself.

Reaching their horses, Stringer tucked the rifle in behind his bedroll and hauled himself up onto his mount. Lagrange used a length of rope to tie the money bags together and drape them behind his own saddle.

Noticing Stringer staring at the bags, Lagrange said, 'I'm sure Ramon would have wanted you to have his share.'

'Ain't about to do him much good now,' the one-eyed man muttered.

Won't do you much either, Lagrange thought, *if that bounty man picks up our trail again.*

Bounty hunters were known for their tenacity. Once they picked up a scent, they just kept coming. If the man tailing them had picked up the woman, he was most likely escorting her out of danger. He would offload her at the first settlement he came across and then double back.

Now, Joe Lagrange didn't like the

idea of a bounty man dogging them, especially if following them led him to their high-country hideout. They had managed to keep it pretty secret up to now, and Lagrange knew that for certain Gallman wouldn't sit easy knowing there was a bounty man dogging their tracks. He would want to go after the man and put him in the ground while they were still well clear of their place. Lagrange saw that as a problem; and being the man he was, he figured the best way to face a problem was head on.

★ ★ ★

When they rejoined the others, a decision was quickly made. Lagrange and Stringer would go after the man and the young woman, and deal with them in the most appropriate way. All the bagged gold was transferred over to Gallman and Wilkerson. It would make travel easier for Lagrange and Stringer. The others would head for the camp upcountry, along with the stolen horse, and Lagrange and Stringer would join them once they were done.

5

The storm fell behind Bodie and Ruby as they crossed the lower open slopes a few hours on. It eased off as quickly as it had started. The swollen clouds began to disperse, and weak sunlight showed through. There was still a proliferation of timber ahead, but for the next couple of miles the way was clear. The open landscape was green with grass and brush, and the horses moved easily. Bodie shrugged out of his slicker, rolled it, and pushed it under his blanket roll. He felt less encumbered with the slicker off. Ruby followed suit.

'Any other time, I would be admiring all this,' Ruby said, staring around. 'All I can think of is Grant and Rafer, dead because of those men. They died for three horses. It didn't need to happen, Bodie. They could have just taken the animals and left, not simply shot down two men who offered no kind of threat to them.'

'It made sense to Gallman and his crew. Dead people can't point the finger and accuse them. And they wouldn't want you being able to tell where they were.'

'So two men were slaughtered to safeguard those . . . those . . . '

'That's the way of it, Ruby.'

'You make it sound so normal.'

Bodie cuffed his hat back, stretching in the saddle as he took a slow look over their back trail. Even though he was expecting problems, it was still a surprise when he saw two distant riders coming down off the high ground in the far distance. In a perverse way, he decided it was almost welcome. His quarry was coming to him.

'What is it?' Ruby asked.

When she saw his backward look, she swiveled in her own saddle. Bodie heard the intake of breath.

'Let's keep moving,' he said.

His mind was working on their best route. During his ride up from the flatland, he had kept a map inside his head, pinpointing landmarks, and he recalled what he had seen now.

'The outcropping to the south. We head for that. Don't push too hard. Ground's going to be soft underfoot from all that rain, so keep your eyes open.' He had his rifle in his hands, checking the load and making sure the weapon was primed and ready.

'Can they hit us from that distance?' Ruby said.

'Let's not wait around to give them the chance to try.'

They moved on, Bodie allowing Ruby to take a slight lead.

★　★　★

'That has to be them,' Stringer said, watching the distant riders on the lower slopes. 'Sonofabitch bounty man.' He jerked his rifle to his shoulder, taking aim, and felt the pressure of Lagrange's big hand pushing the barrel down.

'Ease off, Josh,' he said. 'Too damn far to hit them. All you'll do is waste ammunition.'

'So what do we do? Let 'em go?'

'Way they're going, they'll hit Kramer's place soon enough. We can cut around and reach there first.'

Elijah Kramer ran a trading post that stood near the banks of a tributary of the Powder River. The post had been there for years and had a welcoming reputation. Kramer was ambivalent when it came to his customers. If they had the money, he would deal with them. Good, bad, or indifferent, Kramer made no distinction. His establishment was open on a permanent basis, providing food, drink, a place to rest, and a safe haven for anyone who called by. The law tolerated him because as an honest man, he offered the same to anyone calling in, and for a financial enticement would offer information. On the reverse side of the coin, Kramer kept his less-than-honest clientele informed about any law in the area. He walked a thin line, but knew he was reasonably safe because he offered what they all wanted. Apart from that, he was a haven of comfort — albeit less than the best — to any traveler. A mutual and neutral necessity in the area. Far from any other ports in the storm, Kramer's provided a need; and in the wild, desolate reaches, it would have been a foolish act to do anything that might close the place down.

Lagrange cut off across the high slope, his partner following, both of them satisfied they would reach Kramer's ahead of the pair they were trailing.

★   ★   ★

When he saw the riders turn aside and vanish from sight, Bodie had a moment of doubt. He was sure they hadn't quit. So that meant they were taking a different route, going for the opportunity to get ahead of him and Ruby. He accepted that his intimate knowledge of the territory was thin. That worried him. The Gallman bunch knew this country. It was where they operated from, so it didn't take a deal to understand they would have knowledge of shortcuts.

He stared at Ruby's slim back as she rode ahead of him. As much as he didn't want to lay blame, he couldn't help but call it bad luck he had happened upon her. Meeting up with her in that cave had added to his problems. Bodie couldn't hold it against the young woman. What had happened to her and her companions had not been her fault, leaving her on her own and defenseless. Bodie showing up had offered her a chance of survival, even though now they were far from in the clear.

As if reading his mind, he heard Ruby say, 'Are they still there?'

'No. They've gone.'

She drew rein, turning in her saddle, her eyes fixed on Bodie.

'Are they trying to cut us off? Taking another trail to get ahead?'

She was sharp, Bodie had to give her that. Too sharp to even think of trying to fool her.

'They know the country better than I do. Could be that's what they're doing. So we need to keep our eyes open.'

'Give me an honest answer,' she said. 'If they have the chance, will they try to kill us?'

Bodie nodded. 'No question about that.'

She placed her hand on the rifle's stock, slid it from the sheath, and laid it across her thighs. 'They'd better do it first time,' she said. 'Don't worry about me, Bodie; I'll give as good as I get.'

Bodie figured she meant every word.

6

Elijah Kramer saw the pair of riders coming in across the flatland to the east. They must have come down out of the distant hills and been on their way towards the post. He stood in the open door, arms folded across his chest, watching until he was able to make the pair out clearly. Kramer sighed when he recognized them.

'My luck must be out,' he muttered.

Joe Lagrange and Josh Stringer. Two of Lew Gallman's bunch.

Kramer was well used to having visits from all kinds of men. Good, bad, indifferent. Men on the run. Riding the owlhoot. Drifters and wasters. Out-of-work cowhands. Looking for a place to rest for a while. As long as they paid their way — though often, if he took to someone because of their circumstances, Kramer would offer a man credit. He knew that in most instances they would pay him back. It might take time, but Kramer figured if you gave a man trust, he would usually honor it. He tolerated them all because he ran an open house.

But even he had his own personal dislikes. Not many, but he did *not* like the Gallman bunch. Kramer found the whole lot of them beyond redemption. He knew their way, and he despised them for it. A bunch of hard, unrepentant killers without a single good bone in their bodies. They were, to a man, simply butchers. So when he recognized Lagrange and Stringer, he saw trouble riding in.

As it was, Kramer was on his own that day. The two Crow Indians who helped him around the place were away visiting family. It left Kramer alone, though he was also glad the Indians were not present. He didn't want anyone else around who might fall foul of Lagrange and Stringer.

Kramer never carried a weapon on

him, though he had them placed around the store where they could be reached quickly if needed. A rifle and two handguns. From where he stood in the doorway, there was, on his right-hand side, a loaded cut-down shotgun. It rested on wooden pegs driven into cracks between the wall timbers. All he needed to do was reach across with his right hand and lift the shotgun off the pegs. It was an old weapon — a Greener, its barrel sawed off to allow it to be employed quickly. Kramer looked after the shotgun, as he did all his weapons. It was cleaned and oiled on a regular basis, keeping the workings smooth and ready. He changed the loads every once in a while so he knew he wouldn't end up with a malfunction. Kramer didn't get involved in firefights very often, but he understood the need to keep his weapon ready. It was too late to discover a fault when the other feller was already making his play. A dead man didn't get a second chance if he messed up his first.

Now Kramer didn't move from the doorway. He understood how Lagrange and Stringer operated. If he stepped inside the door for no apparent reason once he had seen them, their minds would shout, *Trap!* They were a touch paranoid in that respect. So Kramer stayed exactly where he was, watching his problem become larger as the pair rode in and halted by the empty corral, tying their horses beside the water trough. Each man took his rifle and stood stamping the cricks out of their legs before they came across the yard.

'Long time,' Lagrange said.

'I'll wager he forgot us,' the one-eyed Stringer said.

'Hell, boy, it was a struggle, but I done managed it.'

Stringer made an angry sound. He might have made a move if Lagrange hadn't placed a massive hand against his chest and held him back.

'Ease off, Josh. The man is funnin,' he said. 'Ain't that the truth?'

Kramer smiled easy, knowing he had

trod dangerous ground. 'Come on, fellers, you know I make everyone welcome. I got a free drink inside.'

Now he deliberately turned his back and led the way inside the one-room post, threading his way between the stacks of trade goods of all kinds to where he had his bar set up. He stepped behind it and watched the pair as they came on. Their eyes searched every corner of the room, checking shadows and searching for any sign of other presences.

'Pretty quiet, Kramer,' Lagrange said.

'That's the way it goes. Come tomorrow I could be seein' 'em piled high.'

'Had any callers today?' Stringer asked, leaning against the bar.

'Nary a one. You fellers are my first in the last couple of days.'

'The storm could have kept 'em away,' Lagrange said. He was still wary; still looking around. He placed his rifle on the scarred bar top. 'Where's that drink?'

'On its way.'

Kramer reached behind him and took a bottle off the shelf, then picked up a couple of shot glasses and placed them down. He uncorked the bottle and poured the whisky.

Lagrange tasted his slowly. At his side, Stringer tossed his off in a quick gesture and held out his glass for more.

'You boys lookin' for supplies?'

'Just lookin',' Lagrange said, and offered nothing else.

Stringer turned around and leaned against the bar. He could see the open door and the spread of the flatland. 'You got food?'

'Yeah.'

'We just rode a distance. Couple of big steaks be nice.'

'Sure. Be a while. I need to get the stove hot.'

'Well, I don't see we'll be going far for a time,' Stringer said. 'Why don't you go get those steaks. And leave the bottle.'

Stringer picked it up and slouched to one of the tables close by. As Kramer turned to go in back, Lagrange joined his partner.

Kramer didn't ask any more questions. He took himself to the kitchen, which was in the back behind the bar area, and set to preparing the food. He stoked up the cast-iron stove and set out the big metal frying pan to heat up. Then he went down into the cool-cellar where he kept supplies and brought up a quarter side of beef. It was no more than a couple of days old, since he had slaughtered one of his own beeves himself for fresh meat. He placed the meat on the smooth slab of wood he used for carving and took one of his heavy butcher knives, cutting off a couple of big thick steaks. Once the pan was hot, he dropped the steaks in, hearing them sizzle as they began to sear in their own juices. He caught each steak and turned them, then left them to slow-cook as he stirred the pot of beans sitting on the stove. Kramer added a measure of molasses to them that gave them a slightly sweet flavor.

The beans thickened slightly as they cooked and would accompany the steaks as a vegetable.

'Hey, Kramer, you got any coffee back there?' Lagrange called.

'I'll bring you some.'

There was invariably a big pot of strong coffee simmering on the back burner. Kramer filled a couple of tin cups and carried them through. He placed them on the table.

'You finished burning those damn steaks yet?' Stringer said.

'Couple more minutes,' Kramer said, and returned to his kitchen.

'I don't trust that dammed German,' Stringer said.

'Why not? And he ain't German. He's from Austria, I heard.'

'Still a damn foreigner. And I still don't trust him.'

'Kramer runs a good place.'

'He'd spit on us given a chance.'

'Josh, you got a weird way of lookin' at things.'

'Right now I'd like to be lookin' at

that damn bounty man 'long the barrel of my gun.'

A couple of minutes later, Kramer brought their food. He put the plates down and handed them eating utensils, then retreated to tidy some shelves. Out the corner of his eye he watched the pair, still nervous in their presence and still trying to figure why they had shown up. He didn't believe it was an innocent visit. Not the way the one called Stringer kept turning to look out the open door.

Damned if they ain't waitin' on someone.

After a time he refilled their coffee, removing the empty plates. 'Food okay?'

Stringer grunted some kind of reply.

'Pretty good,' Lagrange said. 'At least your steaks don't move around on the plate.'

Kramer's eyes strayed to the open door. He saw a pair of distant riders heading in the direction of the post. Stringer must have seen them at the same moment. He reached across the table and tapped Lagrange's hand. The big man slowly swung his head around.

'Yeah,' he said quietly.

His eyes turned and he stared at Kramer. The expression in them made Kramer's skin crawl. He knew why the pair were here now. They were waiting for the two riding in. For an instant his eyes travelled to the shotgun pegged beside the door. The Winchester behind the bar. They wouldn't do him any good. Lagrange and Stringer were too alert to be caught napping.

And there he'd been thinking it was going to be a quiet day. It just went to show you couldn't know what was coming.

7

'Horses beside the corral,' Ruby said.

'I see them.'

'They could belong to anyone, though.'

Bodie only looked beyond the trading post, his eyes picking up the line of tracks coming curving in from the east.

'They came from the north. Cut around east, then into the trading post. Most likely a shortcut that let them get ahead of us. Like I said, these boys know their territory.'

'Only two riders.'

'The others have most likely gone to home.'

'Unless they're behind us waiting to box us in.'

'It's a thought,' Bodie said, 'but I don't think so.'

'Bodie, they could pick us off right now.'

'Then do exactly what I tell you. Don't question. Just do it.'

She looked at him with defiance in her eyes, and it seemed she might refuse. 'I . . . '

'I don't need to be worrying about you if things get serious.'

'All right. I get the message. Just tell me and I'll do it.'

'Soon as we reach the water trough there, I want you out of your saddle and flat on the ground. Get your head down and stay there. Just keep your rifle handy. If I signal, don't wait. Start shooting.'

They closed the distance. Bodie had the feeling they were being watched. He kept his Winchester flat across his thighs, ready to respond. He scanned the sides of the trading post, searching for any movement that might show. There were no telltale signs anyone was concealed, but Bodie never took anything on face value. He slid his finger across the rifle's trigger, watched the water trough come close, and slipped his boots out of his stirrups.

The door to the trading post showed as a dark oblong. Bodie saw nothing at first. Then he picked out a moving shape just inside the door — faint, staying to one side; then the merest gleam of light along metal . . . a gun barrel.

'Now, Ruby — get down.'

Out the corner of his eye Bodie, saw her slide from the saddle and drop flat behind the trough.

He pushed her from his mind after that as the gun barrel was shoved forward, muzzle hard in his direction. Bodie took long steps as soon as his boots hit the ground, away from the chestnut, his rifle arcing up and settling on the doorway.

The rifle there fired. The slug plowed into the soft earth, kicking up a dark jet. Bodie came to a halt, his own weapon returning fire. He worked the lever, triggering fast, and sent out a trio of .44–40 slugs. Long splinters of wood exploded from the door frame. Bodie saw the rifle barrel jerk back, lost in the shadow inside the doorway. He changed direction, charging directly for the timber wall of the trading post and bracing himself there. The door was on his left. He could hear a man cursing, and picked up angry words.

' . . . of a bitch. Burned my damn shoulder . . . I'll cut out his miserable heart . . . '

Bodie glanced in the direction of the water trough and saw Ruby peering around the end. He raised his rifle and gestured with it in the direction of the door, hoping she would understand. He made a circular motion with his hand and started towards the far corner of the building. Behind him, he heard the crash of shots as Ruby began to lay down a volley aimed at the doorway.

Bodie slipped around the corner, moving quickly along to the far end. He was banking on there being a rear door, most likely leading to the kitchen area. Over his head he could see smoke issuing from a chimney stack rising above the roofline. There were no windows in the side wall. A long stack of cut logs stood against the wall, and he had to step around them as he reached the corner, pressing against the wall as he peered around. He could still hear the shots coming from Ruby's rifle. She was spacing her firing so not to empty her magazine too quickly.

Along the back wall, Bodie saw the detritus from the trading post: piles of rubbish, empty boxes, trash. The smell of decay. He saw the rear door standing open. The aroma of cooked meat drifted out through the opening. Bodie went in fast, moving to the side to avoid being silhouetted in the opening.

'Sonofabitch come in here,' a voice yelled. 'Back way, Joe . . . '

Bodie heard the scrape of boots on the hard-packed floor. Something clattered and a bottle shattered as it fell. A dark shape appeared around the edge of the bar fronting the kitchen area.

'I see him!'

The crash of a shot sounded. The

slug clanged against a cooking pot hanging from a hook and howled off the thick metal.

Bodie ducked low, feeling the heat radiating from the cook stove close by. A second shot sent more lead in his direction.

The shooter reared up, swinging his rifle back and forth. He had a lean face showing cheekbones, with graying hair and a black patch over his left eye. It was enough of a description to tell Bodie who the man was.

Joe Stringer. Another of Gallman's bunch.

Stringer spotted Bodie and turned fast, following through with his gun. Bodie lifted his Winchester and triggered his shot a second after Stringer fired. The outlaw's slug clipped Bodie's shirtsleeve and went on to embed in the far wall. Bodie's shot hit, slamming into Stringer's right shoulder. He yelled and stepped back but refused to lower his weapon. Bodie hit him again, levering and firing, sending a number of slugs into the man's body. The final slug slammed in between Stringer's eyes and blew out a bloody chunk of bone as it exited. Stringer staggered back, torso starting to glisten with blood from the multiple wounds.

Bodie laid the rifle aside and drew his handgun. The rifle could be a hindrance in the confines of the building. He moved quickly from the kitchen and around the bar.

A crumpled shape lay on the floor: Elijah Kramer, blood streaming down his face from where a gun barrel had struck him. A few feet away was the hulking figure of Lagrange. The moment Bodie emerged from behind the bar, Lagrange lifted his rifle and fired — and missed, the slug chunking into the wall behind the manhunter. Lagrange pulled the trigger again. The rifle failed to fire — faulty cartridge or empty breech, Bodie never knew. He brought his Colt on line. Lagrange's powerful arm swept back, then forward again and he hurled the rifle at Bodie, who attempted to duck. The rifle slammed against his right arm and hand, knocking the pistol from his fingers.

Lagrange gave a wild roar and sprang forward, far faster than a man of his bulk was meant to move. He slammed into Bodie, smashing him against the edge of the bar with force enough to drive the air from his lungs. Lagrange wrapped his huge arms around Bodie and held him in a bear hug, squeezing Bodie's ribs and making it hard to breathe.

And Bodie knew he had a fight on his hands . . .

8

He was unable to get his hands free, his body overwhelmed by Lagrange's huge bulk. The man lifted Bodie's feet clear of the floor and shook him like a rag doll. Bodie could feel his chest compressing. He was barely able to suck in air to keep him from passing out. He knew he had to break Lagrange's hold quickly before he passed out.

From the far distance, he heard Lagrange's voice: ' . . . killed Vasquez . . . now you shot Josh . . . goddamn sonofabitch, I'll squash you like a bug . . . '

The way things were going, Bodie could have agreed with what the man was saying. There were few options left open to him. Bodie swung his head back, then forward, butting Lagrange directly over his nose. Lagrange felt the pain as his nose broke and blood streamed from it. He shook his head, spraying blood in all directions.

Bodie repeated the move, putting in every ounce of strength he could muster — once, twice, a third time. Lagrange's nose was reduced to a bloody pulp, cartilage crunching. Blood slid in a bright torrents down his face, into his open mouth as he sucked in air. He felt the man's bear hug slacken as Lagrange succumbed to the blinding pain. He forced his own arms apart, breaking Lagrange's grip; and the moment his feet hit the floor Bodie gave himself working room. He sank his bunched fists into Lagrange's stomach, brutal blows that made the man gasp. A further blow over Lagrange's right side delivered with unrestrained force.

As Lagrange stepped back, Bodie slammed in a left, a right, another left to his jaw. The blows were brutal, snapping Lagrange's head back and forth, pushing him across the floor. Bodie kept up the barrage, reducing Lagrange's face to a crushed mask of split flesh and streaming blood. He was aware he had to stay on top. If Lagrange turned the fight around, it might have a different outcome.

That was exactly what the man did. His powerful arms swung up to stop Bodie's blows, pushing them aside, and leaving the manhunter briefly open to the attack. Big fists swept in, clouting Bodie across the jaw — left, right, left again. The blows hurt, and Bodie stepped back to stay out of Lagrange's way. He might have succeeded if he hadn't lost his footing and went down on one knee.

Lagrange gave a snuffling grunt and hurled himself at Bodie. He caught the manhunter as he came upright, his heavy bulk slamming into Bodie and driving him backwards. Bodie caught the edge of one of the tables, stumbled and fell across it, and Lagrange let his bulk slam down on him. The table swayed and collapsed under their combined weight. Bodie felt his breath being crushed out of him as Lagrange's body sprawled on top of him.

They struggled briefly, each seeking the upper hand, until Bodie spread his hands and brought them together with full force over Lagrange's ears. The big man grunted and jerked back. Bodie slammed a fist into Lagrange's exposed throat. The man began to choke, spitting blood that had streamed from his nose into his mouth. Bodie twisted his body and managed to tip Lagrange sideways. The moment he was clear, Bodie scrambled to his feet and leaned in; and as Lagrange started to rise, he slammed in a couple of brutal blows to the man's already blood-streaked face. Bone cracked in Lagrange's jaw.

Bodie slammed in more punches before his opponent could recover. Lagrange fell sideways and Bodie drove his boot into his side, over the ribs. Lagrange gave a grunt of pain. He almost went to the floor, but with a tremendous surge of strength he drew himself to his feet, shaking his great head. Blood sprayed from his face. His thick jaw was askew, pulling his mouth into a crooked snarl as he held himself upright. Bodie had set himself, fists clenched tight; and as Lagrange struggled to regain his balance, Bodie slammed in more blows to the man's stomach, bending Lagrange forward, his head presenting itself for Bodie's next barrage of solid blows that sent him crashing to the floor.

Lagrange hit hard, and for a moment it appeared he was finished; but then he rolled and came to his knees with surprising speed, his right hand dropping to the Colt holstered on his hip as if he had only just realized he was wearing it. As the pistol came free and Lagrange swung it around to track Bodie, the manhunter threw himself aside, hearing the crash of Lagrange's shot. The slug gouged a chunk out of the hard-packed floor.

Bodie kept moving as Lagrange rose to his full height, left arm sleeving blood from his eyes as he leveled the Colt again. Bodie twisted his body across the floor, right hand reaching for the Colt he had dropped. As his fingers

76

closed around the butt, he heard Lagrange's second shot and felt the tear of the slug across his side. He thrust out his arm, tilting the muzzle up and put a slug into Lagrange as the man dogged back the hammer for a third shot. The slug thudded into Lagrange chest high and was followed by three more. Lagrange went over like a felled redwood, his body landing hard.

Bodie stood, hand pressed to his side where blood was seeping through the bullet burn in his shirt. He leaned against the bar, sucking air into his aching lungs. He saw a bottle on the bar and picked it up, pulled the cork, and took a long swallow. The raw whisky brought tears to his eyes and burned all the way down.

After a couple of minutes, he crossed to the door and called Ruby's name. She pushed to her feet, still cradling the rifle, and walked to where he was waiting. She saw the spreading blood-stain on his shirt and the streaks from his mouth.

'Is it safe now?' Bodie nodded and she said, 'And I see you managed to get yourself shot.'

'Thanks for the sympathy.'

'Oh, you know what I meant.'

Bodie led the way inside. She averted her eyes when she was confronted by Lagrange's sprawled body.

Bodie had crossed to where Kramer was stirring, holding a hand to his bleeding head. 'Help me get him in a chair.'

They did, Kramer slowly coming to after Ruby brought water and a cloth for his wound. He stared around, taking in the bloody body. 'There were two of them,' he said.

'The other one's in your kitchen,' Bodie told him.

Ruby glanced at Bodie. 'You killed both of them?'

'They weren't in a talking mood,' he offered.

'And they didn't pay for the food I cooked,' Kramer muttered.

★ ★ ★

It was fully dark by the time they were able to sit and rest. The bodies had been moved to the lean-to outside. The horses were seen to. After Ruby had tended to their wounds, Kramer insisted he cook them food, Ruby helping him.

Ruby had cleaned the bullet burn in his side, seeming to find a moment of humor when she reminded Bodie how he had done the same for her. 'Do you think we'll have matching scars?'

Despite himself, Bodie grinned. Over everything else, she had an open way he found interesting. Ruby had worked on the head wound Kramer had received after being pistol-whipped by Stringer. The trading-post owner had resented the way the two men had abused his generosity and tried to step in when the ambush had threatened Bodie and Ruby.

Bodie sat with a mug of whisky-laced coffee, considering his next move. It was clear what he had to do. Lew

Gallman and Lang Wilkerson were still riding free and he needed to pick up their trail again. In all the years since he had started to track men, Bodie had never walked away. Three of the Gallman bunch were dead. He still had two more to deal with. He would stay at the post overnight, then move on, retracing the way he had come down off the high ground, and locate the tracks left by the two surviving gang members.

He would leave Ruby here at the post, and that would enable him to move faster, without her safety to concern him. Though that wasn't strictly true. Unwittingly, she had been drawn into his world, and he felt a degree of responsibility towards her. It was down to him to make sure she was kept away from further danger, and he was determined to make certain that happened.

9

Gallman and Wilkerson spent the night in a stand of timber, where they made a fire and brewed coffee. As soon as it was light, they checked their horses, refreshed themselves with coffee, then broke camp and mounted up. They were climbing into high peak country now. Looking back, they were able to see the sprawl of timber and brush thickets. Over the stark heights, clouds moved in lazy arcs across the blue sky. The air was starting to take on the sharp freshness that only came at such an altitude. The horses picked their way over the steep slopes with care. They knew were close to their destination now.

Lang Wilkerson leaned forward in his saddle to ease the pressure on his spine. 'You figure the boys are on their way?'

'Mebbe so,' Gallman said. 'Just taking their time.'

The last time they had seen Lagrange and Stringer had been when they had handed over the gold bags picked up the cave where Vasquez had died. The pair had turned about to follow the trail heading down the mountain slope. Wilkerson wondered if *taking their time* was the case. He hadn't forgotten the way Vasquez had died. Getting the drop on the Mexican meant there was someone down there with a quick hand.

'Hope so,' he said in reply to Gallman.

'If they ain't back come tomorrow morning, I'll send Charley Crow. Let him earn his keep.'

Charley Crow was an Absaroka Indian who scouted for Gallman and looked after the gang's base. The tribe had been given the name 'people of the crow', interpreted from the French. Charley Crow, his name a simple affectation by the outlaws, had allied himself to them because he knew the Bighorn range better than most and was able to move around faster than any white man. He saw a better way for himself with the whites, especially Gallman's gang, and so he looked after their hideaway, and hunted for food and ran errands for them. It gave him a place where he had shelter and food and drink. Charley might have given the impression of being harmless, but in truth he capable of killing if the need arose, which it sometimes did. He was a good man with a variety of weapons, preferring a traditional bow to a rifle, though he always carried a .45 caliber handgun as a backup weapon. And as long as he was kept supplied with tobacco and rum, which he liked far better than whisky, the Indian did whatever he was asked.

★　★　★

Hours later, they were traversing the narrow winding pass that took them into the secluded basin through a deep cleft in the towering rock face, where they made their base camp. There was a sprawling log and stone building built against a sheer rock wall, with a corral and a couple of outbuildings. A constant spring provided fresh water that spilled over into a rocky basin and created a shallow stream that meandered across the area. There was grass and timber. The walls of the pass gave shelter from high winds, though during the winter months snow often cut off access and exit.

Smoke rose from the main chimney of the house. A number of horses milled about in the corral. As they neared the house, they saw the stocky figure of Charley Crow forking out feed for the animals. He stopped to watch them cross the final stretch and draw rein next to the corral.

'Where the others?'

'Vasquez is dead,' Gallman said as he dismounted. 'We had some problems. Lagrange and Stringer went looking for the man who caused it.'

'They ain't come back from searching yet,' Wilkerson said.

'Come daylight tomorrow, if they ain't back, I want you to go trackin' for them. Follow our trail and pick up where they split from us. Go find out where they are.'

The Indian simply nodded. Gallman knew he need say no more. The Crow would be gone by the time they woke in the morning.

'We have any visitors while we been gone?'

'Couple. Kris Lubbock and Jake Dawson inside. They rode in two days back. They got trouble too.'

Gallman was unloading the gold bags from his horse, Wilkerson doing the same. 'Hell, I can't ever recall when Kris wasn't in trouble,' he said.

'He attracts it like flies 'round horse shit,' Wilkerson said.

'Charley, see to the horses and bring our gear inside.'

'Sure 'nuff.'

They trooped in through the door and dumped the bags of coins on the big table in the center of the room.

'That coffee smells good,' Wilkerson said.

'It do.'

Across the wide room, a door opened and a tall lean figure stepped into view, tucking a bright green shirt into his pants, his thick corn-colored hair hanging to his shoulders. He peered at Gallman and Wilkerson with sleepy eyes. 'Boys, you make noise enough to wake the dearly departed.'

Gallman looked the man over. 'Hell, Kris, in your case it looks like it worked.'

Kris Lubbock blinked a few times to bring his eyes into focus. His brown face, wrinkled from sleep, was unshaven. 'That you, Lew? Damned if it ain't.' He met Gallman in a couple of long strides, reaching out a big hand to take his friend's. 'Been a while.'

As they shook, Wilkerson turned from the coffee pot, a mug in his hand. 'Kris.'

'Now there's an ugly face I ain't seen in a long time,' Lubbock said.

'Not likely to forget.'

'I hear you boys been running a nice game in these parts.'

Gallman jerked a thumb at the bags of coins on the table, grinning. 'We like to see money gettin' distributed evenly.'

'I'm all for that. Where are the rest of your boys?'

'We run into a little hassle. Picked up a feller on our trail.'

'Law, or maybe a bounty man,' Wilkerson said. 'I'd say bounty man. Law don't like comin' up here.'

'Lagrange and Stringer went back a ways to see if they could pick up tracks,' Gallman said. 'While earlier we ran into a couple of strangers. They had a woman with 'em. We put the men down but the woman gave us the slip. Signs say she and this feller been following us headed back down the mountain. Seemed the thing to go after 'em in case they spread the news we was in the area. Woman saw our faces, too. We had this place to ourselves a good while. Don't want no law pokin' around.'

'If the lawdogs get a sniff, they might start lookin' close,' Wilkerson said.

Lubbock helped himself to coffee. 'Got to protect your place. You want we should stay around a while in case you get unwanted company?'

'Who you got riding with you?'

'Just the one,' Lubbock said. 'You know Jake Dawson?'

'Jake — hell yeah. Last I heard, he was down Tucson way.'

'We partnered up six months ago. Done pretty good until we almost got caught a couple weeks back when we hit a bank over to Casper. Had to run pretty fast to lose a local posse. They backed off after a couple days. I figured we should stay low for a while, let the smoke die down.'

'You are surely welcome,' Gallman said. 'Could always use an extra gun if things warm up.'

Charley Crow came inside with the gear he had taken from the horses. He put it in a corner. 'You want food?' he asked.

Wilkerson said yes they did, so the Indian made his way across to the corner of the cabin where the cooking was done on a squat iron stove.

'Charley's goin' to track our boys tomorrow. See if he can find out where they are,' Gallman said.

'Charley, if you're cooking, better throw something in the pan for Jake,' Lubbock said.

'You got it.'

Jake Dawson put in an appearance the moment the food was put on the table. He was a skinny bearded individual who was losing his hair. Steel-rimmed spectacles, with thick lenses that enlarged his eyes and gave him the studied appearance of a hoot-owl, were perched on his nose. He wore untidy loose clothing that dangled from his boney frame, and knee-high flat-heeled boots. In a waist-high cross-draw rig he carried a Remington 1875, .44 caliber revolver. Despite his weak eyesight, he was a good shot, and more often hit his target than missed.

He grunted an acknowledgement when he recognized Gallman and Wilkerson, then sat down and helped himself to the food Charley Crow had delivered on a huge wooden platter.

'Talkative as ever,' Wilkerson observed.

'You know Jake. Only talks when there's somethin' worth sayin',' Lubbock said.

Later, Gallman tipped out the coinage from the bags and set to counting what was there. The others lounged around, discussing anything that came into their minds, drinking coffee and smoking, tipping a whisky bottle that was passed from hand to hand.

Charley Crow squatted in his favorite corner near the log fire kept burning in the stone fireplace while he cleaned his pistol and made sure his bow was ready for use, the hide quiver held over a dozen feathered shafts. When he had those weapons to his satisfaction, he took out the knife he carried and sat working it on a well-used whetstone until the edge was sharper than any razor.

'That boy looks like he's ready for business,' Lubbock observed.

'And you'd be right,' Wilkerson said.

'When he rides out come morning, he'll be on a killing trail,' Gallman said, glancing up from counting the coin.

*   *   *

By the time first light came and the sun dispelled the mist that had crept down from the higher peaks, Charley Crow had already gone. He had woken early, saddled his black and white pinto, and left without disturbing any of them.

He picked up the tracks Gallman and Wilkerson had made riding in and settled in as he made his way. He knew it blindfolded. This was his land, and had been for decades, before the white men came; and Charley Crow rode easy.

He felt the warm sun and breathed the fresh air of the mountains. The Crow Mountains. Let the whites come as they may. This was still the land of

91

his father and his father's farther.

It was Charley Crow's land. The land of the Absaroka.

10

'Bodie, you don't have to do this. Why go after these men? Look what happened already . . . '

Ruby watched as he continued checking his weapons, thumbing in fresh loads. He did it with the sure hand of someone so familiar with them it came easy.

'Mr. Kramer — Elijah, can't you make him see sense?'

Kramer raised both hands in defeat. 'You see what those men did here. If they're not stopped, how many others will suffer? When I tried to interfere, I almost ended up with my head caved in.'

'You men and your pride,' Ruby said. 'I . . . I can't reason with you.' She turned and walked out of the trading post.

'A very strong-minded young woman,' Kramer said. 'You think she has a point, Bodie?'

'In her eyes, she figures I'm going at it wrong.'

'She can only see her friends being killed in front of her. Enough death for any young woman to have to live with.'

Bodie stood, pushing back his chair. Even though he moved carefully, he felt the painful reminder of the bullet crease in his side, despite Ruby having cleaned and bandaged it from Kramer's medical supplies. He understood it was going to be sore for some time, and didn't have the luxury of waiting for it to heal. The longer he waited, the further away Gallman and Wilkerson were going to get. Time was not on his side. He had already delayed his departure, resting overnight at the post. Now with morning brightening around them, he decided it was time he moved.

'Elijah, you going to be comfortable me leaving her here with you?'

Kramer smiled. 'A beautiful young woman under my care? I love the company, and she'll be fine. My Indian friends will be back tomorrow. Between us, we'll keep her safe.'

Bodie crossed to the door and stared up at the distant peaks. The sky had taken on a clear, refreshing appearance. He felt Kramer move to his side. 'Weather won't be any problem,' he said. 'I don't see any more storms coming.'

'You certain about that?'

'I've lived here for many years, Bodie. I know these hills. I know the weather. If I tell you wrong, you can come back and shoot me.'

'If you *are* wrong, I might just do that.'

'Hey, go make your peace with the lady. I'll go sort out your supplies and make sure you have everything you need.'

'Good luck?'

'That you will have to supply for yourself, my friend.'

★ ★ ★

Bodie found Ruby with his horse, busy checking the saddle and trappings. She had her back to him, and her slim shoulders were taut under the new shirt Kramer had provided. She made no attempt to face him when he came up behind her.

'They got to be stopped, else others are going to die,' Bodie said.

'Why does it have to be you?'

'It's what I do best.'

She turned suddenly, and the first thing Bodie saw were the tears running down her cheeks.

'Damn you,' she said. 'What if you go out there and get yourself all shot up and . . . ' Bodie felt himself pushed back when she leaned against him, gripping him with her arms. 'I can't let you get killed as well. I already lost my cousin and the man who was guiding us.'

'Difference Is, I do this for a living, Ruby. Doesn't guarantee I can't get hurt, but I figure I stand a better chance. I understand men like Gallman. It gives me an advantage.'

'And you think that justifies putting yourself in danger? Bodie, I can't believe you do it just for the money.'

'Comes in handy when I need to eat.'

'So hard,' she said, her tone slightly mocking. She turned her face up to stare at him, a flush coloring her cheeks. 'Back home this would be considered shocking . . . ' She kissed him on the lips, and there was nothing ladylike or chaste about it. 'You see, it matters what might happen to you. It matters a lot . . . '

11

Charley Crow had worked out the mix of tracks he'd found. He judged the freshness and the way one set merged with another, giving him an indication where the different parties had moved. He had spent some time on his haunches, inspecting the overlapping hoof prints until he was satisfied he understood. He backtracked and found the cave where the body of Vasquez still lay. He stood over the dead man, more than a little sorry the Mexican was gone. Vasquez might have been part of Gallman's gang, but he was still a *foreigner* in the eyes of the others, just as Charley Crow was. A part of the group who was still apart. When he left the cave, Charley Crow cast around and found where Lagrange and Stringer had ridden a different route that would eventually take them to the trading post run by the man named Elijah Kramer. The way they had ridden would get them to Kramer's ahead of the pair they were following.

Charley Crow took the direct route, wondering why there was no sign of Lagrange or Stringer returning from Kramer's place. It was a new day, and they should have been on their way back to rejoin Gallman — unless they had run into more than they could handle. He accepted that the pair were well able to look after themselves; yet it was possible something might have happened to them. He didn't like to think that way. On the other hand, Charley Crow knew bad things could happen, so he rode with his bow in his left hand with a nocked arrow, just in case.

He rested his pinto and took time to taste some of the rum from the bottle he always carried with him. There were times he admitted his liking for the drink was not wise. As with much of his race, Charley Crow was easily affected by it if he took too much, but he always felt he could conquer that weakness. As he rested, he took another couple of swigs from the squat bottle, enjoying the warm feeling that spread through his body. When he put the bottle away, he ignored the slight hesitation in his movements and mounted up again before moving off.

* * *

He sighted the trading post from his concealed position in a stand of timber and brush. It stood open and exposed, the creek flowing some way behind it. Charley Crow tied his pinto, then eased through the greenery and settled down to study the layout.

Smoke rose from the post's chimney. There were horses in the corral. Charley Crow's attention was drawn to a pair. His keen eyes identified them as the ones ridden by Lagrange and Stringer. If the horses were here, it told the Indian the riders were as well.

Figures appeared, stepping outside the post. Charley Crow instantly recognized Elijah Kramer. He had seen the man many times before. There was a bandage wrapped around Kramer's head. The unmistakable shape of a young woman appeared. She was talking to Kramer.

A second man appeared. Tall and leanly muscular, he wore a tied-down Colt and carried a Winchester rifle in his hand. He spoke briefly to the woman and Kramer, then crossed to the corral and saddled up a chestnut mare. Kramer handed him a sack that he tied behind his saddle, and led the horse out. Charley Crow studied the man's face, a faint stirring at the back of his mind. It came to him after a minute or so.

He was looking at Bodie. The bounty man known as the Stalker.

Some years back, Charley Crow had seen the man at a rendezvous on the banks of the Green River. He had heard talk the bounty man was on the lookout for a known killer. Charlie Crow's interest had been surpassed by his need to make his own deal for furs he'd trapped and he forgot about Bodie, though he did learn later that the wanted man had been shot and arrested by the bounty man. Last heard, Bodie was taking his prisoner back to Laramie. Charley Crow had never crossed paths with him, but now it was looking as if he might.

Charley Crow saw the man looking at the tracks his friends had made riding into the trading post. Bodie, still talking to Kramer, gestured back and forth as they talked. After a time, Bodie spoke to the woman, mounted his chestnut, and picked up the tracks that showed where he and the woman had left on their approach to the post.

He was going after Gallman and Wilkerson, retracing the way he and the woman had ridden in by. Bodie would follow those tracks to where Gallman had broken off and headed up into the mountains. The bounty man was no fool. He would follow those tracks until they led him to the high camp where Gallman would feel safe. Only, Bodie was not to know there were two more men there to side Gallman and Wilkerson. He would be facing four men, not two.

Charley Crow waited until Bodie was well out of sight, the timber hiding him from sight. That didn't worry him. He would let Bodie ride away and follow him. Let the manhunter believe he was riding alone. Then Charley Crow would deal with him. He would show Gallman the way it should be done.

By a warrior. By Charley Crow of the Absaroka tribe. Always.

12

The feeling he was not alone persisted. Sixth sense. A premonition. Even the smell of something in the air. Bodie held his relaxed position in the saddle. He was over an hour out from the trading post, closer to two, doggedly following the distinct trail left by himself and Ruby. He still had a way to go before he reached the location of the cave where things had begun. It seemed a lifetime had passed since then. It was alarming how quickly events could overtake a man and turn his life around. Yet right now he needed to put all that behind him and concentrate on what was building.

He knew he had acquired a shadow. Someone who was following him, concealed in the trees and brush close by. Bodie hadn't spotted anyone yet, but he knew he was there — someone who had picked him up after a few miles, at a discreet distance but definitely present. Someone Bodie didn't know. Nor did he know the reason why he was being trailed. All he did know for certain was the real presence, and sooner or later he would find out who it was. The tracker was good. He knew the way to play the game, but gave himself away a couple of times — whether by clumsiness, or by some perverse design. Whatever the reason, Bodie kept his counsel and let the rider follow on.

He slid his right hand casually to rest against his thigh, then down to the holstered Colt, neatly slipping the hammer thong free. His Winchester was close, the butt rising from the leather sheath.

Bodie didn't enjoy being followed. Not knowing why simply added to that feeling. He halted the chestnut and reached for his canteen, taking a slow drink. While he did so, he filtered the sound coming from close by. The movement of leaves, stirred by the light breeze. A creak from a tree branch. The flutter of wings as a bird launched into the air. They were normal sounds. Bodie drew them in and dismissed them, listening for something not normal. His tracker had made such small mistakes that they would have been passed over by anyone else. Like the faintest creak of leather as someone shifted position. The softest breath from a waiting horse. Easily missed if you were not paying attention.

But the manhunter was. Over the years, he had developed the ability to pick up on oddities; sounds that were easily overlooked by someone not attuned. He depended on that skill. It had saved his life on more than one occasion.

And it was about to do so again . . .

* * *

Charley Crow felt the slight tremor in his hands and flexed them impatiently. He knew what caused it. Too many sips from his rum bottle. It was his own fault and there was no one else to blame. He had taken a couple too many; and his system, unused to the potent liquor, rewarded his foolishness by taking his sharpness down a notch or two. Charley Crow corked the bottle and twisted round to push it deep into his saddlebag pouch. He felt the pinto start at his sudden move and he quickly hauled back on the reins to bring it back under control.

He took his eyes off the man he was trailing for a few seconds. A brief mistake, but that was all it took.

Bodie caught the closing shape coming up on his left side, emerging from the greenery that fringed the slope he was riding across. Briefly exposed as he crossed the shallow slope, Charley Crow almost failed to see the horse and rider off to his right, breaking from a stand of timber. He saw them but was too late to pull back. The rider had to have seen him.

Charley Crow raised his bow and took swift aim. He gripped the pinto with his muscular thighs as he lined up the arrow. The second he let his arrow fly at the rider, he jabbed in his heels in to urge the pinto forward, reaching for a second arrow as he did.

Bodie heard the hiss of sound as the arrow burned the air close by. It thudded into a tree just beyond him. He saw the black-haired Indian mounted on a pinto pony as the rider used his legs to guide the animal and set himself to loose off another arrow. The moment he let fly, Charley Crow slid from his pony and ran for cover, knowing he was a big target on the pinto's back. He crashed through the thicket growing around the trees, half-turning to loose another shaft that flashed by Bodie's chestnut.

Snatching his Winchester from the saddle boot, Bodie kicked free of his stirrups and rolled out of the saddle. As his feet touched the ground, he slapped the chestnut on the flank and gave a yell that spooked the animal. It ran clear, leaving Bodie in the open. He turned his rifle on the spot where the Indian had vanished and triggered a four rapid shots into the greenery. The .44–40 slugs chewed and slapped at leaves, and tore chunks of bark from the trees.

The brass casings were still in the air as Bodie took a long dive, sprawling full-length on the ground. He levered and fired a couple more shots into the thicket, then rolled to the right and pumped a couple more shots into the timber.

Charley Crow had not been expecting such a speedy response. The chestnut's rider had left his saddle, dropped and returned fire with barely a pause. As the Indian pulled back, he heard the fusillade of shots; heard the whine and crack as the slugs peppered the timber. He had the sense to crouch low and stay down until the shooting ceased, though he knew it would start up again if the white spotted where he was.

Nocking a fresh arrow, Charley Crow peered through the tangle of the thicket, eyes searching for any sign coming from the white. He saw the man's horse some yards off, grazing, but there was no sign of the man himself. A sheen of sweat beaded Charley Crow's face. He acknowledged the man had proved he was good. It made Charley Crow realize the white was no novice, which made him a man to respect. Still a man to kill, but one who would be worthy of an Absaroka warrior.

Easing back into the trees, Charley Crow circled around, aiming to move in from the side after he had gained some distance. He was in no hurry. A man who rushed his moves was simply asking for trouble. He slid easily between the trees, through the thicket, his passing making barely a sound. His skill at moving unobserved did not fail him. Charley Crow was as good now as when he had been a younger man.

As a true Absaroka, he carried the legacy of his people, who had run free in this land before the white men came; and though the strength of the tribes had been reduced, those who remained still carried the warrior spirit. Gallman and his men treated him like a servant, and he took whatever they threw at him. Because it suited him. Because there was little else left for the people of the crow. So Charley Crow did their biding, even their killing — but only because it suited him at this time.

Charley Crow froze. He had picked up a sliver of sound to his right, in the open beyond the fringe of the trees. It was not a natural sound. Not a noise of the Mother Earth. So it had to have come from the white. He was close.

Only Charley Crow's eyes moved, separating the light and shade, seeking what was not part of the land. Something alien. Not even an animal, because he would have recognized the sound it made in its passing. So this had to be the white, who was showing much patience. Charley Crow allowed a smile to edge his lips. There was no shame in praising an enemy; and this man, Bodie, had shown himself to be just that.

He raised his bow and drew back on the arrow, because he had seen the motionless form in the gently moving brush. He focused his eyes and drew down on his target, hearing the bowstring sigh as he put it under pressure. The seasoned wood creaked slightly as it bent.

Charley Crow had to move to clear the tangle of the thicket. Just enough to give himself a clean shot at the white.

* * *

Bodie had made out the Indian's presence as he lay stretched out on the ground. He watched and waited, his rifle in both hands, held sideways on until he chose his moment to fire. The indistinct form, sheltered by the thicket and the half-light in amongst the trees, offered him a poor target. He wanted — needed — a clearer shape. Not a figure in shadow, broken up by the tangle of intertwining foliage. If he fired too soon and only wounded the man, the Indian might be able to slip back into deeper cover, losing Bodie any advantage. This had to be a clean shot, because Bodie didn't want to have to go into the thicket to draw his man out.

So he bided his time, aware the Indian was most likely doing exactly the same thing — watching *him* and waiting until he had his shot. Each man wanting his moment to come, yet holding back lest he fire too soon and miss . . .

★　★　★

Charley Crow felt the tension in his arm and shoulder muscles from holding the bow ready. In his younger years, he would hold such a stance for long periods, maybe waiting until a deer strayed into the right position for a killing shot, so he could release his arrow and take the animal down. Then his shots were clean and sure, the barbed flint arrowheads piercing and sinking in deep. The same applied when he was firing on an enemy. A true arrow would end a man's life with certainty. Yet now, though the spirit was strong, the flesh was weaker. Charley Crow understood this. He admitted his years were slipping by and his body was not as powerful as it had been. And he knew the poison of the rum he had been drinking was also weakening his strength and his resolve.

You must do this, because you are of the Absaroka. Still a warrior and better on a bad day than any white you stand against.

A bead of sweat ran down Charley Crow's brow and stung one of his eyes. He clenched his teeth.

He leaned out a few inches further and dropped his line of fire, then made a final pull against the tenseness of the bow and released the arrow. He heard it sing as it flew, and felt sure he had his kill . . .

★ ★ ★

The shape emerged from deep cover, head and shoulders, a drawn bow in his hands. The angle of the Indian's body suggested he was aiming directly at Bodie.

He responded in kind, gathering his legs under him and pushing to his knees, the Winchester sweeping round to target the man.

The arrow came slicing through the air between them.

Bodie fired. He felt a wrenching shock as the arrow hit the Winchester's wooden stock. The rifle was knocked out of his hands.

Out the corner of his eye, Bodie saw the Indian jerk back a step as the .44–40 slug hit his left shoulder. The bow dropped from his grip.

On his feet, Bodie snatched his Colt from the holster, hammer snapping back as he moved forward.

Charley Crow felt the stunning smack of the slug as it hit his shoulder. His fingers opened and he let go of the bow. He reached for the pistol in his belt and drew back the hammer.

Okay, he thought, *let that sonofa-bitch stand up to this. I can play the white man's game.*

He always cross-notched the lead slugs so they made big messy wounds when they hit. So if he did hit the white man, he would go down hard. No doubt on that score.

Bodie saw Charley Crow go for his handgun. He pushed his own Colt forward and fired, seeing the slug impact against the Indian's chest. Charley Crow stumbled, his pistol going off and sending a slug wide. Bodie hit him a couple more times, the .45 slugs pounding his body. One blew out his spine in a shower of blood and gore. Charley Crow's legs simply collapsed under him, and he pitched down on the ground.

Bodie moved to stand over him, smoke drifting from the muzzle of the Peacemaker. 'Lost your touch there, Chief,' he said.

'That arrow would have skewered

you, white man, if your rifle had not gotten in the way.'

'Might have. Could have. It didn't. I ain't about to get into a sweat over maybes.'

Charley Crow started to cough up blood, his body trembling from shock. 'You are not going to get Lew Gallman.'

'Got three of his boys already. Now you. I'm cutting the odds pretty close. You boys are not so tough after all.'

'Lagrange and Stringer at the trading post? They are dead, not captured?'

'They pushed their luck too far.'

'I saw the woman there.' Charley Crow stared up at the man towering over him, eyes narrowed against the light. 'And I know you.'

'Yeah, I'm the feller who just shot you.'

'Back a ways I saw you at a Green River rendezvous. Few years back now. You were hunting then. I remember. Damn bounty hunter . . . for money . . . '

'Certain sure I ain't doin' it for the

good of my health.' Bodie shucked out the empty casings and reloaded the Colt, never trusting enough to take his eyes off Charley Crow.

'You waiting for me to die?'

'Makes no difference to me. I ain't got paper on you, so there's no reward.'

A gleam of recognition shone in Charley Crow's eyes. 'I heard you caught up with Silverbuck a while back too. That right?'

'Right enough.'

Charley Crow's lips curved in a bloody smile. 'Could be Gallman's in for a surprise then.'

Bodie slipped his reloaded Colt back in his holster. He heard a soft sound come from Charley Crow, and when he looked again the man had died, eyes wide open and a smile on his lips.

'That surprise . . . ' Bodie said. ' . . . Gallman could die from it as well.'

13

Lang Wilkerson went across the cabin and stood looking out across the basin. He had a bottle in his hand and kept taking gulps of the raw whisky. His mood was becoming increasingly dark. He leaned against the door frame.

'Something ain't right,' he said, his words beginning to slur.

'That's what you been saying for the last couple of hours,' Gallman said. 'Gettin' a little tedious there, Lang.'

Wilkerson turned around, his face flushed — mainly from the whisky, and waved the bottle. 'Well excuse me all to hell for being worried about our friends.'

'You think I'm not?'

'Don't exactly look to be so.'

Lubbock and Dawson, engaged in a hand of poker, heard the conversation. They stayed out of it. This was something between Gallman and Wilkerson, and it wasn't done to step into a private argument. So they kept their heads down and stared at each other over their cards.

'Those boys know how to handle themselves,' Gallman said.

'So did Ramon. You forgot he's dead?'

'No,' Gallman said in a calm voice, 'I know Ramon is dead. Had to happen to one of us sooner or later. Jesus, Lang, we ain't going to live forever. None of us. It was Ramon's time. Could easy happen to you or me. We chose this business, and it comes with risks. Ask Jake. Ask Kris. They'll tell the same. Their luck went south, and that's why they come here — to sit it out until things cool down for them.'

'Yeah, but they ain't had anyone killed.'

'Not yet,' Lubbock said, seeing a way into the conversation. 'That bank we busted, well it turned into a regular shootin' gallery. Lucky for us those pen-pushers hardly knew one end of a gun from t'other.'

'They was bustin' caps all over,' Jake Dawson said. 'Could have been one of us took a bullet if they'd not been so scared.'

'Scared?' Lubbock managed a grin. 'They wasn't the only ones. Tell you, Lang, we scooted out that town like cats on a hot tin roof. We come that close.'

'Never rode so fast, so far,' Dawson said. 'Damn it, Lang, we moved so hard we outran our own shadows.'

Wilkerson swayed back into the room. He dropped onto one of the wooden benches at the table and grasped his bottle in both hands, staring with hazy eyes at Gallman. 'You figure they'll be okay?'

'Take a damn good man to beat 'em,' Gallman said.

He didn't know it at the time, but it *had* taken a better man.

And his name was Bodie.

* * *

He didn't bury Charley Crow. He neither had the time nor the inclination. Bodie dragged the body into an overhang of brush and pushed the dead man's bow in alongside him. Then he took Charley Crow's handgun and tucked it behind his belt. Picking up his Winchester, Bodie stared at the arrow sticking out of the stock. He worked the arrowhead out of the wood and tossed it aside. He examined the wood, relieved that although there was a hole, the stock wasn't split. He took out his knife and shaved off the ragged edges of the damage. Next time he was in the vicinity of a gunsmith, he would have the stock replaced.

Bodie saw Charley Crow's pinto tied up in amongst the trees. He led the horse out into the open and dumped the saddlebags on the ground before he stripped off the full trappings, setting the pinto free with a hard slap across its rump.

His own horse was grazing close by, unconcerned. Bodie slid his rifle into the saddle boot. When he went through the Indian's saddlebags, the only useful thing he found was a hide bag of .45 caliber bullets, which he placed in one of his own saddlebag pouches, along with the Colt he had tucked into his belt. Additional firepower was always handy.

There was a brown bottle of rum. He left that where it was. Bodie didn't take to the liquor. Rum always left a mealy taste in his mouth. That was all he found except for a number of tribal items — the Indian's medicine cache. If the man had been expecting them to offer him a charmed life, they hadn't exactly worked this time around.

Mounting up, Bodie cast around until he found Charley Crow's trail, where he had headed down in the direction of the trading post. He saw where they returned and moved into the stand of timber where Charley Crow had waited for Bodie. He sat and studied the hoof prints for a time, then swung the chestnut around and began to backtrack.

He had no idea how far the man had come. That didn't concern Bodie. He had his way in front of him. All he needed to do was follow it back to where Charley Crow had started from. He was pretty well satisfied he would find Lew Gallman and Lang Wilkerson at the trail's end, and as far as Bodie was concerned that was all he needed.

★　★　★

As smart as Charley Crow had been, there was one thing he couldn't do. That was to eliminate the hoof prints his pinto had made, which Bodie was thankful for. By late afternoon, he had backtracked the Indian to the cave where Vasquez's body still lay. By this time, the corpse had been visited by wildlife and was not a pleasant sight. The only good thing about the cave had been meeting Ruby Kehoe, and Bodie concentrated on that rather than the body.

From the cave, Bodie had seen the

tracks left by the Gallman bunch, those of Lagrange and Stringer breaking off as they headed away, while the others had ridden off in the opposite direction. He fell in line with the signs, moving north and taking to the higher slopes, until daylight faded. Then he made camp and built himself a small fire so he could cook himself a meal and brew coffee. With darkness, the temperature dropped and Bodie shrugged into his coat. He sat nursing a second mug of coffee; and without even consciously thinking of her, the image of Ruby came into his mind.

Ruby Kehoe.

The young woman from back East. Though not exactly out of her depth. From what Bodie had learned, she had done some traveling with her cousin. She had an adventurous streak a mile wide. It had been bad luck to have run into Lew Gallman and his bunch of killers. Her escape had saved her life. Despite the threat to her, she had kept her head; and even if Bodie hadn't shown up, there had been a chance she might have survived.

Without knowing it, she had made a distinct impression on Bodie. He didn't dismiss the pleasant thoughts he experienced when they formed. They came easily, and he realized that had to mean something. Though they had been together only a short time, the memory lingered. She was more than just beautiful. Something in her stubborn personality had struck a chord in Bodie — her determination to stay strong despite what had happened to her. Spirited and sharp, the young woman refused to back down. He decided to seek her out after he had dealt with the Gallman bunch. There was no guarantee she would reciprocate his interest, but he was at least going to make an effort.

By the time he finished his coffee, Bodie picked up on the wind soughing down through the timbered slopes. It was not strong, but it carried a chill that was to be expected in this high country.

Glancing up through the branches, he saw there was a bright moon with clouds scudding by. He wondered if another storm was brewing. He pushed to his feet and checked out the chestnut, which had been ground-tied within the timber so that it was as protected as he could make it. Bodie took his saddle and dropped it near his fire, unrolled his blankets and spread his slicker over the top in case it did rain. Then he poured the rest of the hot coffee into his mug and settled down under his blankets. He worked the ground under him until he was comfortable, finished his coffee, then laid his head on the saddle.

★   ★   ★

He woke at first light and found that his concerns about the weather had been unfounded. When he kicked off his blankets, he saw a clear wide-open sky. The early-morning chill was already disappearing. Bodie got his fire going and heated up fresh coffee. He downed two mugs, cleared away his cooking gear and rolled his blankets, tying them in place once he had saddled the chestnut.

'You ready to go to work?' The horse swung its head to look at him, curling its lips. 'Well, good morning to you. I only asked.'

He stroked its muzzle. The chestnut nickered softly, pushing against him.

Bodie spent a couple of minutes checking the horse for cuts on its legs. It didn't take up much time but it was worth it to satisfy himself the animal was fine. He made a final check on the saddle, making sure it was secure, before he climb up. Gathering the reins, he turned the horse out of the trees and picked up the tracks he'd been following the previous day.

The morning spread around him; and despite the reason he was up here, Bodie had to admit it was good country, wide and green with timber and brush. He was climbing steadily now, the slopes taking him higher in towards the distant peaks. The main Bighorn range still lay in the far distance, and on the uppermost of the peaks he could see some snow. Bodie wasn't too worried about that. It was too early in the year to expect snowfalls even up here. In fact, as the morning wore on, he felt the warm sun on his back. It was not the searing heat of the desert, but a pleasant enough feeling that was a welcome change from the raging storm that had plagued him a couple of days ago.

Bodie couldn't prevent the memory of walking through the rain into that cave, seeking shelter and being confronted by Ruby Kehoe and her Winchester. It had been a defining moment for them both, culminating in their ride through that storm until they had reached Kramer's trading post. And even that had been nothing like the peaceful refuge they had expected. Lagrange and Wilkerson had been there ahead of them, laying in wait.

Bodie banished the thoughts and cleared his head. He needed to concentrate, not dream about the past. Somewhere ahead of him were the men he was seeking. They were his priority. Letting himself be distracted was simply asking for trouble.

14

The tracks faded, then reappeared as he hit rocky areas. At this height, the dense treeline had all but vanished, leaving granite slopes and towering escarpments. Vegetation became scarce as well — patches of brush; here and there a thicket. Bodie was forced to backtrack a number of times to pick up some faint marks on the rocky strata. He dismounted more than once to check out what turned out to be nothing more than natural markings in the rocks. Then he found an isolated depression where a hoof had touched a patch of soil between slabs of stone. Crouching, he inspected the marks, working out which way they were going. It was time-consuming, but Bodie had been practicing his tracking skills for a long time and his instinct told him to trust his judgment. He found sign that riders had passed this way, back and forth, the most recent he judged to have been from the pony the Indian had been riding when he went on his search for the missing men. That would have been Lagrange and Stringer.

A further distance on, Bodie picked up tracks which showed that a pair of riders had moved towards higher ground, driving the stolen animals as they went. They ran almost parallel with those of the departing Indian.

Lew Gallman and Lang Wilkerson heading for . . . Bodie stood observing the tracks, tipping back his hat as he scanned them. 'A man could get himself in a tangle working out these damn tracks, horse,' he said.

The chestnut turned its head at the sudden sound of his voice. It pawed at the ground with a hoof, restless at the long standing. Bodie picked up the dangling reins and led it off, eyes following the faint lines of tracks.

He reached an open stretch where the seemingly unbroken rock gave way to dark, coarse earth where patches of mossy grass grew. The tracks showed clearer here; light maybe, but he was able to follow them with little effort. They led more or less north, up into the heights, and Bodie realized he was in for a long climb.

Abruptly the tracks angled off into a wide ravine with steep rock slopes on either side. The base of the ravine was covered with more earth, with hardy thickets dotted along its length. It meandered its way for a couple of miles. Bodie eased himself back into the saddle and let the chestnut make its own pace.

The air at this high altitude was a shade under being cold, despite the sun overhead. Bodie estimated it to be late afternoon now, so he still had a few hours of daylight. There was no telling how much further he might have to go. The ravine ahead made a wide curve to the right; and when the chestnut negotiated the bend, Bodie saw a grove of stunted trees and brush. He saw the horse's head come up and felt it pick up the pace, and saw why after a couple more minutes.

There was a glint of water in amongst the greenery, flowing down the ravine side and forming a natural pool where the rock surface at the base had been worn into a pan. The water filled the hollow, spilling over and soaking into the surrounding area. In the south, the Mexicans called these pans *tinajas*. Bodie called them a godsend. He could see where the bunch of horses had watered, milling around to leave a mass of tracks before moving on again along the ravine. He slid from the saddle, taking his canteen with him, pulling off the cap and emptying the warm water out so he could refresh it. The chestnut needed no encouragement. It nudged him aside as it made for the pool, dipping its muzzle and drinking deeply.

'Excuse me,' Bodie muttered.

He stepped up to where the water spilled from the worn cleft in the rock and let it flow into his canteen. When it was partway full, he took a drink himself, the cool liquid easing his dry throat, then continued to fill the canteen. He splashed a handful of water over his face, feeling his unshaven jawline, then took off his hat and ran a wet hand through his thick hair. He turned and watched the horse as it continued to drink. Moving to it, he picked up the reins and led it away from the water.

'Enough,' he said. 'Fool animal, you'd drink until you had a swollen belly.'

The chestnut grumbled but let Bodie move it well clear. It dipped its head to crop at the grass sprouting from the watered ground near the pool. Bodie let it feed for a few minutes while he moved around to ease the kinks from his body.

He wondered what he might eventually find at the trail's end. Something told him it would be a permanent camp where Gallman and his bunch could retreat when needed. A hidden place where they felt secure, well away from regular trails. Staring up at the rocky escarpments made Bodie aware of the remoteness of the area. There were a hundred places a group of men could retreat to and feel safe from pursuit. The mountains offered a safe haven for those wanting isolation. The great towering crags and peaks would provide just that. From such a place, Gallman could lead his gang out in any direction they chose, descending to the flatlands and then striking where and when they wanted. Pursuit might follow; but with the law spread far and wide, Gallman would fade away in the empty hills, and from there back into his mountain lair.

Gallman's way had proved successful so far. Only, now the outlaw bunch had a shadow following them. Bodie. He sought out his quarry and did what he did best — became the Stalker. The tenacious bounty hunter who picked up the scent and stayed with it to the end.

His legend had grown over time without Bodie having any hand in it.

He simply did the job he was best suited for. The stories got around by word of mouth, and as with most they were embellished with each telling, growing beyond the original facts. Bodie took nothing from them — apart from the unwelcome attention they sometimes brought him. There were those who decided he was fair game himself. The ones who had the urge to establish themselves as hard men. In their eyes, taking down a man like Bodie was worth the challenge. Bodie had no time for glory seekers, whether they were wanted men or simply individuals looking for the accolade that would go to them if they succeeded. He never advertised his skill with the gun he carried on his hip. It spoke for itself whenever he had to use it, but he understood it attracted a certain type, desperate to prove themselves. As far as Bodie was concerned, they were sad individuals desperate to gain the *notch* on their guns. Faced with a direct challenge, he would do his best to talk his way out — but if that failed, he was never going to step away.

The way ahead became harder, the chestnut having to put in extra effort to overcome the steep rise. A couple of times Bodie had to dismount, hauling on the reins to keep the horse moving. There was no other way to go. The faint track marks on the weathered stone led him on, forward and upward. In places those hoof marks became increasingly visible where a horse had slipped on the rocky surface. It convinced Bodie he was on the right way, and he coaxed the chestnut to keep moving. The feisty mare showed her displeasure a time or two, and Bodie had to talk her round.

'At least it ain't raining on you now,' he said. 'Nice warm day, so quit playing around.'

The slope eventually leveled out and Bodie let the horse stand for a while. She was blowing noisily, mostly for effect, so he ignored the tantrum. The mare, seeing her ploy wasn't working, calmed down and stood waiting.

Bodie saw where a number of scuff marks on the rocky surface came and went. It suggested a coming together where riders joined and left the immediate area. He led the horse and began to make a close inspection. He saw the tracks were all moving to and from a high rock face. The weathered escarpment rose hundreds of feet overhead. Here on this high point, the wind became stronger, lifting dust and chipped detritus. Bodie followed the thin trail, keeping in close to the vertical wall. Some scrub grew at the base, and Bodie might have missed the narrow cleft if he hadn't been watching close.

It was no more than six feet wide. A split in the eroded rock face, and it appeared to run deep into the escarpment. All the hoof prints he had been following went into the cleft. Bodie stepped inside the opening and found more tracks in the accumulated dirt running ahead of him. He stood and inspected the marks. Ahead, the passageway into the rocks ran in a crooked line that began to widen as it faded into shadow, the top of the cleft coming together so that it formed a tunnel shape, closing out the light. He studied the passage for a while before retreating and moving outside.

Bodie stepped back from the rock face and stared up. He saw immediately there was no way to climb the wall. It rose to a dizzying height. He realized if he wanted to get inside the escarpment he would have to use the tunnel. That added its own problems. It was an unknown, with what appeared to be little in the way of concealment if someone decide to traverse it while he was there. If he was going through, he needed to pick a time when it was less than likely others would be thinking the same. He figured that meant a night incursion. Even that might have its own difficulties, but Bodie couldn't see any other way he could do it.

He turned and took up the reins, leading his horse away from the cleft. He wouldn't be going in on the chestnut. He was going to walk in.

Bodie made the cover of a thicket some four hundred yards away. He led the chestnut into it and tied her to a low branch. He tipped water into his hat and let the mare drink her fill, then took a long swallow himself from the canteen. There was some grass for the animal to feed on.

Taking his Winchester, he checked it was fully loaded, then did the same with his Colt. On impulse, he took the second pistol from his saddlebags and loaded that too, then tucked it under his belt. His final action was to make sure the razor-sharp knife was secure in the sheath on his left side. He had favored the knife ever since he had taken it from the half-breed gun for hire Silverbuck. He had used it to cut the breed's throat — twice, in fact, because the man had survived the first time and had spent a long time searching for Bodie to have his revenge. He almost got it. They had finally met in the desert below Yuma and had once again fought for survival. When Bodie walked away, he knew the breed wouldn't be coming back for a third try. He had made certain Silverbuck was good and dead that time.

The light was fading fast now. As night slid over the peaks, stars starting to show, and Bodie saw a pale moon shining. He checked the chestnut for the last time, stroking its glossy coat.

Bodie settled down himself, with his back against a mossy rock, stretching his long legs out. It was peaceful now, with the only sound coming from the grazing mare and the low sigh of the constant wind. He let himself relax, knowing that he might need to expend a degree of energy once he set himself to walking.

This was a moment of calm before the coming storm, which he knew *would* come once he encountered Gallman and Wilkerson. They would not give up without a fight. Bodie never even considered they would hold up their hands and surrender. They were of the hard breed — men who made their own rules, stuck to them and never gave in. They had chosen their way long ago. They offered no easy way out to anyone who stood in their way. Killing came easy to them. It was the rule they clung to all the way down the line.

Kill them before they kill you.

Back east, the thin veneer of civilization held society together in a way that was still struggling to exist here on the frontier. In many instances, men made their own rules in order to survive. There was little choice. The country was vast; much of it still untamed. The law might work in the established towns, but once men stepped away from them they were left to settle their differences by their own hands. Lawlessness offered more chances for those who shrugged off society. Men who took what they wanted from others because they could. Men like Lew Gallman and his crew. Men who were too idle to work for their rewards. It was easier to let others do that, then step in and steal it; kill for it without regard for their victims. It was by any criteria a savage way to live. Yet it suited Lew Gallman and Lang Wilkerson. It had been the same for the others. Lagrange. Stringer. Vasquez. Charley Crow. All of the same breed.

Now Gallman and Wilkerson were the only ones left. Unless there were others at their hideout. Bodie had been working on the assumption he only had two to deal with. What if he was wrong?

He might be letting himself in for an unpleasant surprise when he turned up to confront the supposed two and walked in on an armed bunch. It was something he couldn't discount. He was going to have to face that possibility and work around it. His idea to move in under the cover of darkness was still his favored thought. It might offer him an opportunity to check out just how many he might be up against, and allow him time to work out his strategy. A thin smile edged his lips. Whatever he decided, there would be a degree of making it up as he went along. He was not in a position to do much else, given the lack of information about the strength of Gallman's bunch. Bodie was never one for worrying too much about the odds. He would face whatever he found and deal with it.

He listened to the chestnut's steady breathing as it settled, and felt in his shirt for one of the cigars he carried with him. There were a few Lucifers wrapped in a patch of oilcloth. He was about to take the cigar out when he stopped. It had been a damn fool notion. The smell of burning tobacco could have been picked up for quite distance. Easy to forget, and allow himself to be located. Men had died for something as small as such a mistake.

Forgoing his smoke, Bodie settled and waited out his time to move.

15

It was still dark when Bodie roused himself, drank the rest of the water in his canteen, took his rifle and slipped quietly out of cover. He judged it to be around four by his internal clock. The quiet time before dawn. He made sure the chestnut was secure. Clear of the thicket, he made his way to the shadowed cleft, stepping lightly. In this pre-dawn time before the world roused itself, the profound silence magnified any sound, so Bodie kept noise to the minimum. When he slipped into the tunnel, the darkness became virtually complete and he was forced to feel his way along. He stayed close the left wall so his rifle remained clear in his right hand. He didn't want to create any sound by accidentally brushing the weapon against the stone.

He could feel the soft earth underfoot

as he moved, treading with caution. For a short while, he imagined he could feel the darkness closing in around him, as if the very stone walls of the tunnel were moving to trap him. It was sheer imagination, he knew, though it took a time for him to shake off the sensation. Perceptions had that habit of creating threats where there were none. In daylight, the confining size of the tunnel would not have concerned him. In the inky blackness it was different. Bodie knew there was nothing there. No phantoms or imagined enemies. Yet he still felt an enclosing sensation; an eternal fear of the dark. Something that had existed as long as man himself.

He felt the tunnel wall curving, telling him it was moving him around a bend. Bodie followed step by step, testing with his feet that there were no unseen holes that might trap him. His slow progress seemed to have gone on for hours. He had lost the ability to gauge the passage of time. All he really knew was he had walked for a long while. He felt the ground underfoot slope down, then level out again. His boots splashed into water, and the hand feeling its way along the wall of the tunnel encountered moisture. Water seeping from the deep levels of the rock. He touched his fingers to his lips. The water was ice-cold. Bodie paused and repeated the action, allowing the moisture to his lips, letting it wet his dry mouth. He cupped his hands to contain more water and drank gratefully. He could feel the chill of the pooled water through his boots as he moved on.

The bend in the tunnel leveled out. Bodie stopped as he realized there had been a gradual change in the pervading darkness. He looked up and saw the walls of the tunnel outlined against a graying sky, fading starlight showing where the roof of the tunnel had opened up again. He would not have admitted to anyone but himself that he felt relief at the sight.

The pale illumination exposed the

floor of the tunnel as the light grew stronger. Bodie took a look behind him. Where the walls had come together, the darkness still existed. He wasn't sorry to be out of that.

The coming daylight brought it own concerns. If Bodie could see, so could anyone ahead of him. His caution forced him to slow his progress, more so as the tunnel itself widened out.

Bodie stayed close to the rock wall as he took the final stretch, coming with surprising swiftness to the end of the tunnel. He dropped to a low crouch, tight in against the wall, and studied the lay of the area confronting him.

What he could see confirmed what he had been thinking. This was where Gallman had his base. A deep, wide basin created by the natural barrier of the escarpment walls. Grass and timber. Water spouting from a spring, feeding into a rock pan, then extending from that into a stream that coursed across the basin floor until it formed a steady pool. Bodie was able to see the timber and stone construction of the extensive cabin, flanked by a corral and a couple of smaller outbuildings. As daylight spread, allowing Bodie a clearer view, he saw there were a number of horses in the corral. He counted at least nine. That didn't mean the presence of nine men. Three of them would be the ones taken from Ruby and her now dead companions. Simply extra mounts in the remuda. The reverse side of the coin might show different. There might easily be more men around, and Bodie didn't discount the possibility.

He studied the layout for a time. He needed to clear his present position; find himself a spot where he could watch the cabin and make his mind up how to handle things. Off to his left he saw a fall of hefty boulders that must have come down from the high escarpment at some time in the past. They lay in an untidy formation, and Bodie saw them as a place to conceal himself. They were at least sixty feet from where he crouched; not a great distance, but to reach their cover he would have to expose himself. He needed to make his move now, before the light became too strong.

Once he accepted that, he moved. There was no point sitting and going over the situation. He eased out of cover, set himself, and ran in a crouched position. He didn't look back; just powered himself across the open ground and held his rifle close to his chest. He tensed himself for the crash of a shot that thankfully never came, and slid into the cover of the rock fall, where he found himself a comfortable spot from which he could look back across the basin and view the cabin clearly.

He saw smoke starting to drift from the chimney formation on the timber roof. A little time later, the main door opened and a man stepped out, a wooden pail in one hand, his thick straw-colored hair falling to his collar. Bodie watched him cross to the water pool and sink the pail, filling it. The man paused to splash water on his face, shaking his head and sleeving his face.

Bodie got a good look at him, and the first thing he registered was not recognizing him. He was not Gallman or Wilkerson. It confirmed the fact there were more than just two people present in the cabin. How many more, Bodie couldn't work out for the moment.

He watched the man return to the cabin with the growing feeling that in the space of a few seconds, the odds had gone up from two to three. How many more were inside the cabin?

Bodie assessed his weapons. The Winchester held fifteen rounds of .44–40 caliber. He had a pair of .45 caliber Colt Peacemakers, each one fully loaded with six rounds apiece. And he had at least that again in his gunrig's belt loops. A fair count if he used them wisely. It went without saying that Bodie was not in the habit of blazing away regardless. He always attempted to gain the maximum hits during any gunplay. It didn't always work out that way, and he would have been the first to admit to that. On this occasion, it would behoove him to contain his shooting until he had a sure target. And he didn't forget his sheathed knife.

He saw the cabin door open again, and this time he recognized the lean figure of Lang Wilkerson as he crossed to the water source and crouched to scoop up handfuls to wash his face. When Wilkerson walked back to the cabin and stepped inside, Bodie was gripping his rifle in tight hands. It would have been an easy shot to put Wilkerson down, but it would have taken away the element of surprise. Bodie wasn't about to give himself away so soon.

He leaned back against a curved slab of stone where he could keep the cabin his sightline. He needed to get himself closer to the cabin so he could check out just how many were inside. It was a plan. The only one he could come up with at short notice. And once he had formulated it, Bodie put it into action.

16

It took Bodie an hour of slow concealed movement to reach the far side of the basin. He kept to the shadows of the fallen rocks, and when they petered out he used the spread of the brush and trees at one point. Every time he saw movement by the cabin, he was forced to stop and drop to the ground. It was frustrating progress, but essential. He had to stay concealed for a long period when one of the cabin's occupants came out and spent time forking out feed for the corralled horses. The man was in no rush. He was one of the strangers Bodie had been unable to identify. The bearded individual wore spectacles. Bodie lay in an awkward position, with a small loose rock under him that jabbed into his ribs. He made no attempt to move it. It was small movements that could catch a man's eye even at a distance, and Bodie was in no position to stir things up yet.

The man finished his feeding and stepped out of the corral, dropping the top bar of the crude gate back into position. He stood for a while and just stared around, then took off his spectacles and rubbed his eyes. He replaced the spectacles and turned back to the cabin. When he opened the door, Bodie caught a scrap of sound coming from inside. Voices. Then the door banged shut, and Bodie was on his own again. When he moved, it was with a sense of urgency, not through panic. More because he wanted to get his business finished.

He reached the outbuildings, more a pair of small sheds, and using their bulk to hide himself Bodie eased around the side of the first one, moved to the door and lifted the wooden peg out of the catch. He opened the door far enough to let himself slip inside, taking a look at what was stored there. All he found was an untidy tangle of old leather harness. A worn and moldy saddle. Bodie eased back outside and took a fast few steps to the other shed. Inside it had the same collection of disused items — more tack, old horse blankets, a broken and abandoned wooden chair.

And a distinct odor he recognized easily. Coal oil. The smell came from a number of rust-streaked metal cans, most likely used as fuel for lamps. The strong odor would have been unpleasant inside the cabin, which accounted for the cans being kept in the shed. When the oil burned, it also gave off noxious smoke . . .

Bodie studied the gallon-sized cans, his mind working, and he turned and searched the interior of the shed again. He leaned the Winchester against the side of the hut, took out his knife, and picked up one of the discarded horse blankets. A few quick slashes and he had a section of blanket in his hand. He wrapped it around a shattered leg from the broken chair and secured it with another length of blanket. Unscrewing the top from one of the coal oil cans, Bodie soaked the makeshift torch. He retrieved his rifle, tucking it under his left arm, holding the torch in his hand. Then he picked up the can of oil and eased open the door.

He checked out the area. No one in sight. Bodie cleared the shed and crossed to the corner of the cabin, pressed himself against the end wall, and put down the rifle again. He felt in a shirt pocket and located the oilcloth-wrapped Lucifers there alongside the couple of unsmoked, now crushed, cigars. He extracted one of the matches and scraped it against the butt of his Colt; and the moment it flared into life, he offered it to the oil-soaked head of the torch. It flamed after a few seconds. Dark smoke billowed out.

Bodie knew he was taking a calcu-lated chance here. He was about to attempt a move intended to drive the men from the cabin. That was if his plan worked. What the hell, he decided. Either it did, or it didn't.

He slid around the corner of the cabin, making for the open-shuttered window next to the door. The only good thing was the absence of glass he might have been forced to break. He paused beside the window and took a quick look inside, catching a glimpse of moving figures on the far side. Bodie didn't waste any more time. He laid the can on the bottom frame of the opening and let the oil pour inside. The cap enclosure was a wide one, so the oil flow was fast. Bodie held on as long as he could, dumping most of the contents before he heard a wild yell from inside the cabin. He let the can fall inside and followed up by dropping the flaming torch inside after it. He turned instantly, retreating to the side of the cabin and snatching up his rifle.

He knew his plan depended on the spilled oil being ignited by the torch. As he broke away from the cabin, he could only hear the rising voices from inside, and he knew he was committed, like it or not. Quickly he cut across the open space, aiming to take cover in the thicket near the water.

He was yards away when he heard a dull sound behind him, and throwing a quick look over his shoulder saw a rising burst of flame behind the window that was expanding, with a mass of smoke showing as well.

17

Kris Lubbock had caught movement at the cabin's single window. As he turned, he saw the metal can resting on the bottom of the frame, oil pouring from it and splashing to the floor, the pool spreading quickly.

'We got trouble,' he yelled.

His warning alerted the others, and they all turned and saw the threat as the oil can dropped inside, still gushing. Before they could fully react, a burning, smoking torch was dropped inside the cabin. It hit the floor, the flames wavering for a few seconds before the rising vapor from the spilled oil ignited and a mass of flame erupted, reaching to the roof timbers and expanding across the pool. The sudden heat was enough to make them pull back.

'Son of a bitch,' Gallman said. 'We got to get out.'

Smoke from the blaze was growing, and they could taste it each time they took a breath.

'Fire's covering the window and the damn door,' Dawson said. 'Jesus, we'll burn up.'

'I ain't stayin' in here to do that,' Wilkerson said. He snatched up his rifle. 'No damn way.'

He took a reckless headlong run for the window, ignoring the burning oil. His sudden move took him through the flames and out the window as he launched himself forward. It was a desperate move that paid off as Wilkerson cleared the window and hit the ground outside, slamming his head against the solid ground. He landed hard, losing his grip on his rifle as he rolled to smother the flames eating at his lower legs and boots. He twisted back and forth, scooping up dirt to smother the flames, aware that blood was streaming down the side of his face where he had opened a gash on hitting the ground.

As he pushed to his knees, reaching for the holstered pistol at his side, he saw a tall figure heading for the cover of the thicket by the water hole. Wilkerson stumbled upright, his Colt leveling. He fired a hasty shot and knew he'd missed, but his anger drove him forward to fire again. This time he saw the figure pause and turn, the rifle he was holding coming up to fire.

* * *

Bodie felt the slug's passing. He hauled himself to a stop and brought the Winchester into play. He had a quick glimpse of a disheveled, bloody-faced and smoke-stained figure, flame and smoke drifting off his scorched pants. The man was hatless, face streaked with dirt, but recognizable as Lang Wilkerson.

'Bastard!' Wilkerson screamed in his rage. He centered his Colt and fired. The slug plucked at Bodie's sleeve.

The manhunter's rifle spoke as Bodie

put two .44–40 Winchester slugs into Wilkerson's body. They ripped in, tearing at flesh and organs, and Wilkerson gave a harsh grunt, toppling to one side. He lay on one side, still gripping the pistol, and Bodie took careful aim and put a third shot into the man's head. Wilkerson's skull split apart and mushroomed blood and brain matter.

Bodie heard a splintering crash and saw the cabin door smashed apart. Figures spilled out into the open from the flame and smoke billowed out.

Moments earlier, as Wilkerson took his dive through the window, Lew Gallman had turned about and directed his two partners to one of the heavy wood benches next to the table. They grabbed it and held it between them, taking a run through the fire and smashing it against the cabin door. The force and the solid weight of the bench had the effect they were hoping for. The wood split, the door driven from its hinges.

Gallman, Lubbock and Dawson kept moving, beating at the flames as they emerged from the cabin. Gallman and Lubbock clawed at the guns they wore, searching for a target, and caught a fleeting glance of Bodie as he crashed through the thicket and trees.

Jake Dawson fell face down, his clothing soaking up the oil. As he struggled upright, his beard and clothes alight and his spectacles lost, he stumbled forward. A shrill cry burst from his burnt lips as he struggled to put out the flames. He could feel the flesh of his face and hands scorching. Without his spectacles, he was unable to see clearly, and in his panic turned half-around and slammed into the door frame. His nose was crushed under the impact and blood streamed down his face. Dawson threw up his hands to his damaged nose, falling back and losing his balance again. He fell inside the open doorway, landing on his back, and was engulfed in fire. Losing control, he thrashed about and simply made things worse as the burning oil ate through his clothing and devoured him. The sound of his screaming carried across the basin.

Meanwhile, slugs tore at the brush and ripped slivers of wood from the trees as Bodie threw himself forward, ignoring the pull and scratch of the vegetation. The cover provided was scant, and he realized it was the best protection he was about to get.

He felt the solid thump as something struck his left thigh. No pain at first — that came later — but he did feel the wet rush of blood and knew he'd taken a hit. He braced himself as his leg weakened and he fell, slamming to the ground with some considerable force, the rifle bouncing from his grasp. He sucked in a harsh breath and forced himself to reach behind for the Colt in his belt. Knowing what was coming, Bodie hauled out his holstered Colt as well, twisting over onto his back as he heard the noise of Gallman and Lubbock pushing into the thicket.

Twelve damn shots, he told himself. *If you can't put them down with twelve shots, it's time you quit the job.*

Through the tangle of brush, he made out a moving figure. Close, but not close enough.

Come on, you sonofabitch.

Bodie wanted to see the whites of the man's eyes.

Both pistols had their hammers back and Bodie's fingers on the triggers as he brought them both up.

The looming figure stepped briefly into view, clear against the backdrop of the open sky. His searching eyes rested briefly on Bodie's face. He saw the raised pistols and his mouth dropped open in shock, because he knew he was staring death in the face . . .

Bodie stared back, recognition in his eyes as he saw Lew Gallman. Then he pulled both triggers. Felt the guns kick back against his grip as they spat out flame and smoke.

Gallman's face vanished, leaving behind torn flesh and shattered bone, then a wash of blood as he fell back without uttering a sound. A pulpy ragged bulge formed on the back of his skull. He hit the ground and his body curled in a reflexive action as he died.

The moment he fired, Bodie twisted and caught a fragment of movement nearby. He lurched to his feet, bracing himself against a tree, and faced the surviving figure as Kris Lubbock moved into view, his pistol sweeping back and forth as he searched for Bodie. Their eyes locked briefly, each recognizing their adversary.

'I should have known,' Lubbock said. 'Couldn't have been anyone else but you, Bodie. Ain't no other man could have stayed on Gallman's trail for so damn long.' His gun leveled, finger already easing back on the trigger.

Bodie leaned forward and Lubbock had to alter his aim; yet he was only a fraction behind when the crash of his shot merged with the response from Bodie, who triggered both his Colts repeatedly, the thunder of his fire rolling out across the basin and echoing off the high walls of the escarpment, even as he felt the impact of a slug from Lubbock's gun.

Kris Lubbock was rocked back by the multiple shots that slammed .45 caliber slugs into him. Blood was welling from the holes in his chest as he went down, a long shuddering final breath escaping from his body as he lay there. And died there.

Bodie saw Lubbock fall as he was hit himself. The pain in his thigh had become less as it was overtaken by the stronger one from the slug that had embedded itself in his side, cracking at least two ribs. The ragged furrow it made sent blood soaking through his shirt, all the way down to his pants. Dazed, he slumped back, half-sitting as he stared around him, half-expecting another challenge until he realized he was the only one still alive.

Bodie realized he could hear his own breath because it had become so quiet after the gunfire. He could smell the drift of powder smoke. He felt suddenly very tired, and let himself slide down to the ground. Warm sunlight filtered through the foliage. The air was cool and the mountain breeze stirred the greenery around him. He lowered the guns he was still holding in his hands.

There was a sudden crackle of small explosions coming from the cabin. That would be from ammunition overheating in the fire. He noticed, too, that Dawson had stopped screaming.

Right then, Bodie wasn't too concerned. He knew he should move. Do something about the wounds he'd received. But he was unable to raise the energy to it. He was feeling comfortable. Warm. And the day around him was slipping away . . . Bodie felt his eyes closing . . . didn't have the strength to resist. It felt good where he was, so he decided he would simply rest for a while . . . just for a while . . .

18

Everything was soft. Under him. Around him. Even the pain was reduced to a respectable level. Bodie was reluctant to open his eyes, because he knew when he did he would be back in that basin with the dead lying around him and the smell of burning wood and human flesh. So he stayed in the darkness, and it was comforting, and he was wondering if he was dead too and this was what it was like.

No, he decided, he couldn't be dead, because if he was, there wouldn't be anything to feel.

Bodie figured then if he wasn't dead, just where was he? Then he heard the voice of an angel, something again he didn't believe in; so if it wasn't an angel it had to be something close. And the voice sounded just like . . . like Ruby . . . but Ruby was back at Elijah

Kramer's trading post and he was halfway up the Bighorn Mountains, lying in the dirt with his blood soaking into the ground.

'*Bodie . . .* ' the Angel's voice called, '*you're awake at last.*'

A gentle touch against his cheek. Soft and silky.

'Hey, Bodie, I'm here.'

That damned angel again.

He struggled to open his eyes, reluctantly drawing away from his dream world. Light hit his eyes and he screwed them up. Let the light fade, then took another look.

Ruby's face swam into sharp relief as she stared down at him, concerned. Those soft lips parted slightly. He smelled soap. A fresh-washed smell. Then the gentle hand again, stroking his face.

He tried to speak, but all that came out was a croaking sound.

'Here, drink this.' She slid a hand behind his head and raised it. Held a cup to his dry, parched lips. Cold, fresh water. It hurt his throat to swallow but he managed it until the cup was drawn away.

'Not too much yet,' she said. 'You need to take things easy.'

Bodie reached up with his own big hand and grasped her wrist, aware of how weak he felt. 'Where am I? How long?'

'Elijah's trading post. Over a week — well, nearer two weeks — since we brought you down off the mountain.'

'How the . . . ?'

'We waited a day after you left, then we left Elijah's people here and he rode with me. Elijah sent for a Crow tracker and he followed your trail. Took us a couple of days. I thought we were never going to find you. The Crow located where you went into the escarpment, and we rode through the cleft. It brought us into the outlaws' camp. And we found all those dead bodies . . . ' Her voice faltered. 'Then we found you, unconscious. You'd lost so much blood; but being who you are, there was enough life left to keep you going. We stayed there for three days after Elijah took out those two bullets. The Indian used Crow potions to help with the healing as much as possible before we brought you back here. They made a travois and hitched it to your chestnut.'

'You brought me back down the mountain?'

'Yes. It wasn't easy, but we did it. Brought you here and put you to bed. Bodie, you had a fever for days. I thought you were never going to get through. Oh, we brought the horses as well. They're all in the corral outside.'

'Our young lady did it,' Kramer's voice said, and Bodie looked around and saw him. He was standing at the foot of the bed. 'She's barely slept since you got the fever. You had it bad. Day and night she looked after you. Washed you to cool you down. Changed your sheets when they got wet. Kept your wounds clean as well. Refused any help.'

'Don't make more of it than there was,' Ruby said, her face colored with embarrassment.

'I'll try and find the words to

say . . . ' Bodie told her.

'No need. After what you did getting *me* to safety, I owed you my life.'

'I'd say we were even then.' He caught her hand and held it in his own large fist. 'Thank you, Ruby Kehoe.'

'You're welcome, Mr. Bodie,' she said, and compounded her words by leaning forward to kiss him soundly.

★   ★   ★

Elijah Kramer proved to be a competent stand-in doctor over the next week or so. With Ruby, he tended Bodie's healing wounds and made sure his patient was given all the rest he needed. When he wasn't around, looking after the business side of the trading post, it was Ruby who administered the nursing, which she did with flair.

Bodie regained his appetite under all this treatment. From the bowls of hot soup he progressed to solid food, and with the passing days his strength began to return. Included in Bodie's aids were frequent doses of medicines brought by the Crow Indians who worked for Kramer. They spoke very little, but made up for the silence by bringing him tribal concoctions Kramer told Bodie would help him. Under Ruby's stern gaze, he took them and hoped they were actually doing him good.

'It doesn't matter what's in them as long as they help,' she said. 'Bodie, you have to trust they know what they're doing.'

'Yes, ma'am,' he answered. He had realized it was simpler to just agree with her. Truth be told, he didn't have the strength to argue.

* * *

'You don't seem in any hurry to get back home,' he mentioned a few days later.

'I suppose I'm putting off the evil hour, having to inform family that Grant's dead. With that in mind, I've realized I no longer have my job.'

'That going to mean you won't be able to earn the money he paid you?'

'Grant didn't pay me. After all, he was family. I worked with him because I enjoyed it. Bodie, I don't have to work. We're a wealthy family, and I stand to inherit a considerable sum from my late grandfather in a few years.'

Bodie had no answer to that. He had never been in that kind of position. He was just glad for Ruby. 'Nice to be rich,' he said.

Ruby sobered and said, 'This talk of money has reminded me about your reward for ... for dealing with the Gallman gang. It was Elijah who told me you might have problems claiming the bounties because of not being able to produce the bodies.'

Up until she mentioned it, Bodie hadn't given a great deal of thought to the matter. He saw the possible difficulty now. No proof/no bounty was the norm. By the time he was fit enough to go looking for those bodies, there would be nothing left except bones and tattered clothing. It wouldn't be the first time he'd lost out on a bounty. It didn't happen often, but Bodie wasn't too pleased when it did.

'I can see you're not happy about missing out,' Ruby said. 'So Elijah and I have come up with a solution. We've composed a letter giving all the details about the wanted men and how you tracked them down. We signed it as witnesses, and when I return to New York my father's lawyer will also witness it. Do you think that will be sufficient to prove your claim?'

'He a good lawyer?'

'Oh, yes, one of the most prestigious in the city. Charles Bainbridge is an extremely influential man.'

'Sounds like it might do the trick.'

Ruby perched on the side of the bed. 'Will you go on another bounty hunt when you're well enough?'

'It's what I do. A job that I have the skills for.'

'And that's what worries me, Bodie. That you go after these violent men, risking your life to bring them in.'

He was about to say something lame along the lines of how it was a dirty job but someone had to do it, when Ruby leaned in close and placed her mouth over his. It was a powerful kiss and took him by surprise. A pleasant surprise, especially when accompanied by her soft body pressing against him, and Bodie decided he was still too weak to fight her off.

So he didn't, and for once he didn't do much in the way of protesting.

★ ★ ★

Three weeks later they were in Laramie, ensconced in the most expensive hotel the town had to offer. Bodie was close to having recovered, but under Ruby's close eye he was still taking it easy. After a leisurely breakfast, he was taking a slow walk to the livery stable where their horses were being well looked after. The horses brought down from the outlaw lair had been presented to

Kramer as payment for all his help. He had made a protest, but Bodie had seen the look in his eyes as he assessed the value of the animals. Ruby kept the black she had been riding.

The day was calm, the sun warm. He felt at peace with the world for the moment, thought there was a restlessness growing in him to move on. Not from Ruby, who was proving to be the best female company he had ever known. He needed action. Something to feed his brain and allow him to exercise his skills. The soft living in Laramie was getting to him. He was wearing new clothing, and Ruby had persuaded him to have his shaggy hair cut and groomed. It pleased her and that pleased him. Yet he still needed something to occupy him.

He was on his way back to the hotel, wondering where she was, when he saw her hurrying down the street to meet him, an expectant look on her face. Long gone were the dirty range clothes she had worn before. Now she had on a dress and all the feminine accessories to go with it. Her face was still beautiful and her hair flowed behind her, shiny and neat.

'Bodie,' she called, unmindful that young ladies were not expected to call out in the street. She was waving her hand at him, clutching a buff telegram paper. The last time she had brought one of those, it had been to confirm that her father's lawyer had negotiated with the authorities and Bodie's claim for the reward for the Gallman gang had been approved. Lawyer Bainbridge lived up to Ruby's promise, and he was able to pick up his money from a bank in town.

'I'd ease off there,' Bodie said. 'You'll bust right out of that damned dress if you're not careful.'

Her smile was almost dazzling. 'What, right here on the street? Mr. Bodie, what are you suggesting?'

He didn't pursue that line of thought. 'I take it you have something to tell me?'

She nodded, her face shining with excitement. 'It's a message from Lawyer Bainbridge. He has an offer for you. Not exactly a bounty hunt. He asks if you'd look for someone who's gone missing. The young daughter of a Chinese friend in New York. An extremely important and wealthy man named Chin Yi Soong.'

'Hold on there. Try speaking slowly, Ruby. Remember I'm just a simple feller from the West.'

Her laughter seemed to fill the street, attracting curious glances. 'That is the last thing you are, Bodie. Now are you going to listen to me?'

'Yes, ma'am.'

'There'll be money on offer, Bodie. I made certain that would be part of the offer. But it's important. Jasmine is a friend of mine as well; a beautiful young woman. She'd gone to visit relatives on the west coast, and had been there for almost two weeks when she simply vanished. No one can find her. It appears she was taken off the street. I believe she's been kidnapped. Jasmine is not a foolish young woman. She wouldn't do anything risky, or fail to keep in touch, unless she could not.'

'Has there been a letter demanding money? Anything like that?'

'Nothing. Her family is distraught, Bodie. Their daughter has disappeared on the other side of the country, and they don't know what to do.'

Bodie took her arm and led her back up the street to the telegraph office. 'Send a message to the lawyer. Ask for everything known about your friend. Description. Any identifying marks. Whatever her family has. Send it now. Then we go and sit down at the hotel and you tell me all about this Jasmine. And I mean *everything*.'

When they stepped out of the telegraph office, Ruby clung to his arm. 'Thank you,' she said.

'Once we have the information, I need you to head back to New York. You stay close to the family. I'll contact you through Bainbridge. No games this time, Ruby. I don't expect to turn around and find you behind me in . . . hell, you said the west coast. But where?'

'Oh, I thought I'd said. It's San Francisco.'

★   ★   ★

And it was in the city by the bay a week later when Bodie, already into his search for Jasmine Yi Soong, met up with the man who would for the second time partner up with him.

His name was Jason Brand.

Books by Neil Hunter
in the Linford Western Library:

INCIDENT AT BUTLER'S STATION

BODIE:
TRACKDOWN
BLOODY BOUNTY
HIGH HELL
THE KILLING TRAIL
HANGTOWN
THE DAY OF THE SAVAGE
DESERT RUN
ACROSS THE HIGH DIVIDE

BRAND:
GUN FOR HIRE
HARDCASE
LOBO
HIGH COUNTRY KILL
DAY OF THE GUN
BROTHERHOOD OF EVIL
LEGACY OF EVIL
DEVIL'S GOLD
THE KILLING DAYS
CREOLE CURSE

BODIE MEETS BRAND:
TWO GUNS NORTH

BALLARD & McCALL:
TWO FROM TEXAS
GUNS OF THE BRASADA
COLORADO BLOOD HUNT
COLTER'S QUEST

We do hope that you have enjoyed reading this large print book.

Did you know that all of our titles are available for purchase?

We publish a wide range of high quality large print books including:
Romances, Mysteries, Classics
General Fiction
Non Fiction and Westerns

Special interest titles available in large print are:
The Little Oxford Dictionary
Music Book, Song Book
Hymn Book, Service Book

Also available from us courtesy of Oxford University Press:
Young Readers' Dictionary
(large print edition)
Young Readers' Thesaurus
(large print edition)

For further information or a free brochure, please contact us at:
Ulverscroft Large Print Books Ltd.,
The Green, Bradgate Road, Anstey,
Leicester, LE7 7FU, England.
Tel: (00 44) 0116 236 4325
Fax: (00 44) 0116 234 0205